MAPLE FALLS 2
MASSACRE 2
SACRIFICIAL LAMBS

4

CHAPTER I

The cool waters of Old Syrup remained still and calm. It had not tasted blood and viscera for almost a year and it grew hungry for it, an uncontrollable urge yearning under the surface calling for the reaper to come. For HIM to come and quench its insatiable thirst.

Heaven only knows what lies beneath the old lake, draining it had been just one of the elaborate suggestions put forward by Sheriff Patrick Russell to the authorities. One of many suggestions that was denied, leaving him irate and bemused at their reluctance to do anything about the 'Maple Falls Problem'. Sheriff Russell had reluctantly stepped into the role after the former Sheriff, Keith W. Windwood had gone missing two years past and had remained in the role to witness the horrors that rolled in with the ice and snow of the last winter season.

Seven missing kids, identified by the blood at the scene of a brutal, bloody aftermath left in a lumberjack's cabin. No sign of any bodies, no signs of life, the winter was a cruel prankster, sent to cover the trail of death with its relentless sheets of virgin snow, concealing below it the destructive trail of the beast that cometh whenever the Tear Drop froze over.

Sheriff Russell sat in a kayak in the cool calm water of the Maple Lake, a tranquil and beautiful place that had become affectionately known as Maple Syrup or Old Syrup. The Spring and Summer seasons had brought with it nothing but sun and frolics as the Sheriff's attempts of banning locals from going anywhere near the place had seemingly failed. He reluctantly stepped back and allowed them to camp, hunt and enjoy the warm waters of the lake as they swam and played until sunset. But he remained a watchful eye, fearful that whatever it was that came to claim those missing kids, would come again.

He sat motionless in the kayak, the winter had slowly started to creep in and he was dressed for it. Wrapped in his goose feather parka and ushanka hat, gloved hands grasping the warmth of a metal flask, something hot seeped from it in a hypnotising vapour, an aroma of coffee and a hint of something else perhaps, something Irish. He quivered with the cold, and brought the flask to his chapped lips that were pursed under a heavy, untamed stubble. He took a sip and the heat filled his mouth and warmed his innards as it travelled rapidly down his throat, it was reassuring and calming. But his eyes, those green eyes that wore the heavy burden of darkened flesh beneath his lids still watched his surroundings, watched and waited.

Last winter almost broke him mentally and every day since those events had been equally tough, losing his wife over the whole affair.

So obsessed with finding who (or indeed what) was responsible for these disappearances had driven a jagged wedge between him and his wife, after several months it had all been too much for Holly Russell to take and she left to live with her sister in the neighbouring town of Hope Springs.

Patrick was broken, but he could not fail those missing kids, those dead kids, he owed it to them, he owed it to Sheriff Windwood and to the people of Maple Falls to find this mad man and put an end to it.

I can't just walk away.

His tired eyes flitted around the lake surveying everything all at once, every movement in the leafless trees, or cry of a hunting creature or the flap of a raven's wing, it was all scrutinised and investigated by Sheriff Russell.

I may have lost everything I had loved, but I won't let that happen to the people of this town. They deserve better than that.

It was the report made by Professor Felix Cumberbatch that had first piqued his interest, believing that this creature, this Beau Tooth, whether he was man or beast still remained a mystery. The Professor had been on the trail of an illusive urban legend known as The Blackfoot, but what he had come across was something far worse. The altercation had left the Professor scared for his life and had hotfooted it back to Studd City with his tail between his legs. The Sheriff had made several phone calls and sent a ridiculous amount of emails in an attempt to make contact with the Professor, but all to no avail. It seemed that Professor Cumberbatch had no intention to return to Maple Falls or talk about what had happened there.

I can't say that I blame Cumberbatch.

Sheriff Russell believed that Tooth was residing somewhere in Blackfoot Ridge and was waiting for the lake to freeze over so that he could venture into Maple Falls undetected to fulfil his heinous acts of savageness. Russell had made several trips to Blackfoot and contacted the town's authorities, which was Sheriff Delaney. She had been cordial at best but soon became fed up with his constant pestering and had told him in no uncertain terms not to come back or contact them again or his superiors would be contacted and they would no doubt have his badge. He had laughed when he had received the cease and desist order, screwing it up into a ball and launching it into the wastepaper basket, only to immediately retrieve it and have it framed in a place of honour on the wall of his office.

I mean, who are they going to give my badge to? Nobody wants this fucking job. My badge is safe, my sanity on the other hand?

He had butted horns with his superiors, their ears closed to his outrageous allegations that a phantom lumberjack was slaying the good folk of Maple Falls. He understood why, there was no evidence, blood yes, always blood, but bodies? Not one.

Yes, horns had been butted alright, but none more than with neighbouring Sheriff Audrey Delaney of Blackfoot Ridge. She believed that he was taking liberties and had called for his gun and badge on several occasions.

Jackass! Sheriff Audrey Delaney, what a jackass! I can understand that I may have ruffled some feathers, but they had to know, I had to have them check. I had to know for sure.

Nothing had turned up, every abandoned cabin in their widespread mountains and forests had been checked and nothing. But Russell refused to believe it and so continued to do daily inspections of the area, some days he would circle the Old Syrup a hundred times in his kayak, hoping to find something, anything.

I can still hear a voice screaming in the back of my head telling me to leave this place, make up with Holly

9

and just start fresh somewhere else. But how do I do that when I know he's out there? Out there ready to kill again when the rivers and the lakes freeze over.

He gazed around at the thick grey clouds above that signalled that the weather was about to change for the worst. There were sounds that met his ears and his eyes flitted back and forth trying to seek out where the noises came from. But his tired eyes met only the black pines of Black Leaf and the Blackfoot Trail, the overgrown twisted branches and thorns of Fisherman's Island and the towering pines that rose skyward from the Maple Woods.

He let out a sigh and with it came the warm air that seemed to be ambushed and wrapped in a cloak of ice creating a cloud before his eyes.

He closed his eyes for a moment and knew his time was up. He gazed into the surface of the lake a flawless mirror shimmering, showing him a reflection he did not wish to see, for he did not recognise the face in it any longer. Old Syrup presented what it wanted you to see, it mirrored the world around it and onlookers thought it beautiful to gaze upon, but what about what was hidden at the bottom of the lake? Why create this false persona for the world to see unless secrets are being hidden beneath its mirrored mask.

He removed his glove and dipped his hand into the water, quickly retrieving it. It was so very cold and flakes of ice shards had started to form within. It was always said by the old locals that live within Maple Falls that winter is never truly here until the Tear Drop River freezes over. That particular event happened yesterday and as he gazed skyward again the first flecks of snow cascaded down and settled on his nose and cheeks. Sheriff Russell had had his twelve months to find Beau Tooth and he had failed.

"I'm too late."

CHAPTER 2

Once again the dead of winter was upon the town of Maple Falls, with the snow moving in quickly to smother it with no remorse or sentiment. The chilling breeze brought with it the ice cold fingers of death, devouring whatever it touched with unrelenting callousness. Sheriff Russell had left the woods behind as day made way for night, he had been out in the conditions far too long and it had taken its toll. There was nothing more he could do but to regroup and make sure things were in place, because Beau Tooth was coming, the Sheriff was sure of that and he had to be ready.

The arrival of winter meant that the Sheriff's ban on hunting and fishing (or any entering of the woods at all for that matter) had gone into immediate effect. Signs had been nailed to the entrances of the woods and around the neighbouring area that anyone caught in the woods during the winter period would be heavily fined. Those ignoring the signs and going against the no hunting and fishing policy could even spend time behind bars.

The Sheriff was serious, but some felt that his actions were excessive and uncalled for. The majority of the town believed that he was just being paranoid. These were the people who had never seen anything to think otherwise, deaf ears to the cries of death that echoed through the woods each winter. Eyes blind to the blood stained snow, their demeanour detached from the reality of what really took place in the town when the snow began to fall. The majority were oblivious to the truth, but it was quite possible that was just how they wanted to keep things. If they were to believe Sheriff Russell's proclamation, then that would be admitting that there were horrors to face and they were unwilling to do so. But some of those within the town, the old guard, knew all too well what awaited them in those woods. Although they remained tightlipped and guarded, always anticipating the worst.

Winter kissed Old Syrup eagerly and by nightfall it was completely frozen over, luring out into the open the town's first pair of offenders to go against the new rules that had been set in place. Several wooden ice shanties, topped with slanted tin roofs that were caressed with a layer of snow, stood on the banks of Old Syrup, warped and barren, left to rot under the conditions for another year. The small two man shanties rose from the bank of frozen mud and snow like the crooked teeth of some old man, decaying and useless.

All but one.

One of those old man's teeth seemed to have become dislodged and found itself in the middle of Old Syrup. The snow and wind attacked it from seemingly every angle as its pitiful construction seemed to hold together purely out of stubbornness more than anything else. Its skis had been chipped free of its mud and ice confines, but they remained stained by the earth they had spent the last twelve months submerged in.

Whoever had freed the shanty had used its skis to move it onto the ice where it now stood, a flickering light illuminating the darkness from its small cracked window.

Concealed away from the blistering conditions that shook the shanty were two men, two retired gentlefolk that belonged to the majority that believed that Sheriff Russell was full of shit.

The pair had waited impatiently for the Sheriff to leave the woods, by pulling Abe Slapawitz's decrepit old dairy truck into a lay-by behind a large pile of freshly ploughed snow. Now the pair of eager ice fishers were on the lake going about their business as they saw fit. It was their God given right to hunt and fish and they were damn well going to do it, no matter what Sheriff Russell had to say.

"Lost his marbles if you ask me." Sniffed Howie.

"You're not wrong." Replied Abe, fiddling with a wax worm as it wriggled away in a futile attempt to flee from the hook on his spool of line.

The pair sat around a perfect circular hole in the ice, which was situated underneath a rickety trapdoor that had been prised open to allow them access to the ice.

A gas lamp gave them light and some warmth as the sluggish stove that was installed a lifetime ago tried its best to kick out some heat, but the kindling was damp and failed miserably. Howie Kendal and Abe Slapawitz remained huddled close together on their foldout lawn chairs trying to stay warm.

"Trying to keep a man from doing what he's meant to do." Growled Howie shaking his head and spitting a wad of phlegm into the circle of ice cold water that glowed bright blue at their feet. The spittle froze immediately and floated on the surface of the water as Abe dropped in his line with the pierced wax worm struggling for its life only to be taken by the bitterness of the lake and joined the wad of phlegm in an icy prison.

"You're preaching to the choir old man. I hear ya." Abe replied.

The pair sat in silence for a while staring at the cool circle of the lake that seemed to hypnotise them. The hole had been made by a hand auger which cut through the ice with less effort than the old tools of the past.

"Glad you still had that hand auger, cuts like a dream." Abe said, wriggling his line to tempt any fishes that may still be braving the conditions below the surface of the ice.

"Aye, it belonged to Elroy Pascoe." Howie pondered for a moment, "I wonder what happened to that old fox?"

"Probably a bear got him." Abe shrugged, "His loss is our gain though, brand spanking new hand auger."

"Yeah, I don't think my old joints would have managed if we'd have had to break out the old spud bar." Howie cackled, flashing the few teeth he had left before spitting into the lake again.

"Could have borrowed Chopper's Tip-up though, that would have made life easier." Abe moaned.

"Nah, those blasted contraptions take all the fun out of it. Sitting waiting for a flag to pop up to tell me I got a bite, no sir, I don't want none of that. I want to be in control of my fishing." Howie griped, "Besides he's in league with the Sheriff, he'd snitch on us if he knew we were out here."

Abe agreed, nodding along with him.

16

"Coffee?" Abe asked, retrieving his line and draping it over his knee as he unfastened the large thermos that sat between them.

"Aye. Still hot ain't it?" Howie asked.

"Yeah, it's still hot."

Abe poured the coffee into two old, stained enamel mugs that seemed to have had as hard a life as the two fishermen. The substance that came out of the thermos was thick and black, more like treacle than coffee, but it was hot and sweet and the pair sipped at it eagerly.

The wind whistled around them and the wooden shell that protected them from the horrendous conditions outside, it creaked and quivered as if each movement could well be its last. The tin roof above their heads shook relentlessly causing an annoying din that neither seemed to notice nor care about.

"It's picking up out there." Abe said gazing around at the roof, the cracked small window fit into the door showed him nothing but a curtain of snow.

"Yep." Howie replied, his old eyes squinting into the cold blue waters at his feet, again twitching the spool to make his wax worm dance and look inviting for passing fish. "Hope I can bag me a northern pike or an arctic grayling, either would make this trip worthwhile."

"What do you really think happened to old Elroy?" Abe asked.

"Maybe old hairy Blackfoot got him." Laughed Howie.

"You sound like Chuck Muchnick!" Abe scoffed.

"Another one that let the woods take him." Howie sniffed, nonchalantly.

The wind swept across the lake and it seemed to grumble underneath them, shaking the shanty with its wrath. It was enough to make Abe stop what he was doing and gaze around again at their confines.

"You've got to have your wits about you out here. Those silly old fools forgot that. It's wild out here, gotta respect that, gotta respect the weather and those creatures that dwell in it. You wouldn't find me taking my eye off the ball out here, no sir. Gotta stay switched on."

"Maybe all that talk is right." Abe whispered, "Maybe there is something out there."

"Don't talk wet!" Howie snarled, "Chuck was crazy, we all knew that. You go chasing monsters and it's only a matter of time before one catches up with ya."

"But what about Elroy? He weren't no crazy."

"No." He shrugged, "He probably ran off with some young dainty, anything to get away from that senile old wife of his."

"Now, that ain't nice, Howie. You know she's had a terrible time of late, since Elroy's been gone missing and all."

"A bear got him, or a cougar, or he got caught in a snowstorm or an avalanche. Any number of things. But there ain't no goblins or ghouls lurking out there I can tell you that."

"I'm not too sure you know." Abe's eyes flitted to the window again, positive that he saw something pass by out of the corner of his eye.

"Well, what do you want me to do about it?" Howie snapped, then spat into the lake once again, with a shake of his head.

The pair sat in silence, but Abe was becoming antsy and jumping at every shadow and every creak now.

"Moaning and gossiping like two old broads!" Howie grumbled, "We came here to fish!"

"Okay, Howie, okay, you're right."

Howie felt a tug on his line and an ugly grin swept across his miserable face.

"Ha Ha! What do ya know, I've only gone and bagged me one!"

There was a thump on the door and the shanty rattled on its skis to the point that the whole structure may just teeter over at any moment.

The pair of them turned to face the door as the tin roof rattled uncontrollably, the window showed them nothing but that relentless shroud of snow. They clung on to each other and dropped their lines into the hole in the ice. As quickly as it started the ruckus was over and replaced by the howling of the wind.

"What was that?" Abe snivelled.

"Just the wind, that's all." Howie snapped, but he didn't sound sure, "Let go of me!"

The pair split away from each other leaving them both feeling embarrassed, Howie's face glowing like a beet.

"Hugging me like some woman. Get it together Abe!"

"Sorry, Howie, it's just I thought I saw..."

"Saw what?" Howie snapped, turning to the window to be faced with nothing but snow, "Shit. That's all there is to see, nothing but shit."

Abe scooped up his mug and sipped his thick coffee through shaking hands, eyes remaining focused on the small window.

"Dropped my Goddamn line now, got to bait up again." Howie sighed, "If I don't bag anything now I'm holding you responsible for it Abe. It will mean that it's your round when we get to Chopper's."

Abe's eyes were wide and frozen when Howie looked over at him, the mug hanging by his lip as his mouth hung open as a gagging sound escaped his throat as if he could not dislodge the words he wanted to say.

"What the hell's the matter with you now?" Howie asked, looking a little bit concerned, "Abe?"

Abe's coffee tipped and trickled down his parka, but he didn't notice, all he did was point at the window and gape in horror.

"What is it Abe?" Howie asked shaking him by the shoulders, he finally followed his quivering finger and saw a horrendous face at the window. The scarred and bearded face of a demon, snow settling on his massive bald head as a crooked smile cut across his hideous face. Warm breath steamed up the glass and when it evaporated into tiny crystals of ice, the face of was gone.

"It's him...he's real." Abe murmured.

Howie had no words as the pair held each other tightly waiting for the inevitable to happen.

They did not have to wait too long as the tin roof was the first item to be removed from the ice shanty. It became lost to the wind and caught in a shroud of snow, the sound of it making contact with the ice below echoed around them causing an awful din that startled them. The snow fell inside the shanty and threatened to extinguish their gas lamp, but the glass globe around it did all it could to protect the flame within. The light escaped into the night and illuminated the falling snow above and there he was, the mountain of a man, Beau Tooth towering over the small wooden shanty as he emerged from the sheet of falling snow. He was only there for a moment, disappearing as the snow consumed him again, he left behind a heinous chuckle that took to the wind and circled them again and again, as if trying to drive them insane.

By the time Howie reached for the hand auger to defend himself it was too late and the heavy bit of a bloodstained axe came hurtling through the brittle door. The shanty was split in half, its structure unable to hold as Tooth stepped inside, as he breathed out heavily, his massive chest seemed to cause the shanty to bow and collapse. Before the pair could blink, the axe was buried quickly into the gawping, horrified face of poor Abe Slapawitz and his head mirrored the parting of the wooden walls around them as he collapsed dead, his head split in two.

Howie backed up, but there was nowhere to go, he managed to fend off two blows from Beau Tooth's axe, with the steel shaft of the auger, but the strikes seemed playful, like a kitten toying with a ball of yarn.

Howie had nowhere to go and a heavy blow from Tooth's axe sent the auger spinning from his grip and colliding with the ice of the lake, skidding and sliding out of reach. He grabbed the thermos and threw it at the monster that stood before him, it exploded on impact as it struck his barrelled chest, hot, thick coffee spraying over him and cascading down his torn flannel shirt. The scolding hot coffee sprayed the face of Tooth, but all he did was smile that crooked grin of his, his cleft upper lip creasing to show the gums and scarred flesh beneath.

"Good God, what are you?" Howie wept as he clambered backwards over the broken remnants of the wooden shanty, unaware of his footing he slipped on the open trapdoor and his leg became submerged in the freezing cold waters of the lake. He gasped in horror from the cold but as he frantically struggled to pull his leg out of the hole he knocked over the gas lamp, which smashed on impact and set his sleeve ablaze.

Howie screamed as the flames took his parka quickly, the goose feather within became engulfed and burst through the material to find tender flesh beneath.

Beau Tooth lowered his axe to his side and watched on as Howie was burned alive, his leg still trapped in the hole in the ice. The monster seemed to be taking sadistic enjoyment in what was transpiring before his mismatched eyes. Howie's face and hair was engulfed next and the sound that erupted from his mouth was similar to the squeal of a slaughtered pig.

Beau Tooth had seen and heard enough and put an end to the spectacle with a well placed axe in his chest, that silenced him and Tooth watched on as the conditions saw to the fire, leaving the crisp black carcass of Howie Kendal burnt and smoking.

By the time Beau Tooth retrieved Howie Kendal's body, his leg had frozen and broken off, lost into the shadows of Old Syrup. Two bodies were hauled onto the back of his ramshackle sledge and then with his meaty hand gripped tightly around a rusted chain he pulled it across the ice and was quickly swallowed up by the falling snow.

CHAPTER 3

A long haul truck rolls along Maple Drive and comes to a halt at the entrance to the sleepy town of Maple Falls. The long haul trailer a flash of royal blue against the white canvas of snow that surrounded it, the word *Bobby's Light* emblazoned on it with a picture of an ice cold bottle of beer. The sun had not long risen (not that you could tell in the winter, not in Maple Falls) but the headlights remained on and pointed in the direction of Crimson, its next destination before it would settle at the depot in Studd City to unload its cargo. A light suddenly lit up the cab and the window slid down on the drivers side and an overweight, bearded man, with a truckers cap peeked out at the gentle flurry of falling snow.

"Woo!" He exclaimed, "It's cold enough to freeze a pair of nuts off a cougar out there."

He slid the window back up and shuddered before turning to the passenger seat where a girl sat. No more than nineteen, a mop of black curls and thick spectacles, but behind the spectacles she wore a fiery demeanour of determination.

"You sure you want to be dropped off here, kid?" The driver asked.

"Yeah, here is fine." She said and began gathering her things and stuffing them into a rucksack and sliding on a thick yellow parka.

He shrugged as though it was no skin off his nose where she was dropped off, but he had heard stories of this place and didn't think it was a place for a young girl to be wandering around alone.

"Always seems to be winter in this place." He sniffed, looking back out of the window.

"So I have heard." She said, zipping up her parka and opening the door.

The cold wind met her rosy cheeks and fought a duel against the warmth being kicked out of the truck's heater. As she attempted to climb down out of the cab, the driver's hand touched her shoulder gently and ceased her progress.

"Are you sure you want to be here, kid. I have heard queer things about this place."

His eyes were filled with fear, but he genuinely looked concerned to be leaving her here as though the guilt of leaving a hitchhiker in the middle of nowhere was just too much.

"What have you heard?" She asked, smiling.

"Lots. None of it good, I can tell ya."

"I'll be careful." She smiled and clambered out of the cab, jumping down from the last step into knee deep snow.

"People go missing here you know." He said, a final word of warning, hoping that she would change her mind.

"I know." And with those words she slammed the door and watched as the truck rolled away down Maple Drive, the freshly ploughed road was as clear as it was ever going to be.

"That's why I'm here."

She gazed at the sign that welcomed her to the town and then at the high street that awaited her, a blanket of untouched snow situated in front of her.

CHAPTER 4

A distant rumbling sound stirred Sheriff Russell awake. He sat in his dingy office, blinds drawn over the windows and glass door, his head and torso slumped over his desk as he groaned. He lifted his aching head, weary eyelids flickering rapidly to free themselves of the discharge that had built up over another night spent in his office. He told himself there was nothing to go home for anymore and most mornings he could be found stirring from a pillow of files and papers, his alarm clock usually the toppling of an empty bottle of whiskey, labelled Hackenschmidt.

Today was no different.

His head throbbed like it was the skin of some drum being played over and over again in a relentless rhythm as if calling for war.

He rubbed at his heavily stubbled face, and eyes that were red and heavy, his hair was longer than it had ever been and was slick with a layer of grease. He leant back in his chair and took in his environment that was becoming an all too familiar routine and sighed heavily.

His first instinct was to reach for the bottle, but found that it was empty so he allowed it to fall into the waste paper basket.

The sound that woke him lingered in the background somewhere not too far away and he tried to ignore it, believing it just to be another hangover from a night spent alone with Mr Hackenschmidt.

He gazed around the dingy office, the walls that had once been decorated with his achievements had been replaced by newspaper cuttings, articles and crime scene photographs of last years strange occurrence, that had seen several people go missing in mysterious circumstances, leaving behind only bloodstains and heartache to show that they had ever been here at all.

He gazed longingly at a framed photograph of his wife and sadness consumed him, he didn't even know he was crying when he picked it up and held it close to his chest. He kissed it and slid it into the top drawer of his desk as if he were embarrassed that she should see him in his current state.

"I'm so sorry, Holly." He whispered as he wiped his eyes.

"I never meant this to consume me, but I have to find him. I have to."

He stood up and he teetered for a moment, feeling light headed and unsteady on his feet, a night on the bottle and no food inside his belly had really taken its toll on him. He steadied himself on the backrest of the chair and stretched out his back, the bones of his spine and neck creaked in reply, almost angry at being disturbed.

He staggered to the window and lifted the blind, immediately regretting it as he was met by nothing but a bright whiteness. Snow was all there was and it shone in his eyes and caused him to retreat back to his chair.

He held his head in his hands and cursed his migraine that screamed relentlessly, knowing deep down that he only had himself to blame.

The distant noise suddenly was no longer so distant, it was outside his door and he peeked through his fingers and frowned at the ruckus and raised voices from the corridor.

"What is going on out there?" He asked himself.

"I don't fucking care if he's busy!" Came the aggressive raised voice of a young woman.

"Can you please keep your voice down, Miss!" Came the reply, the voice he knew was his Lieutenant, a good woman who had tried to look out for him since he had hit rock bottom. Tammy Adams had a soft spot for Sheriff Russell but he didn't know that, he wasn't in any shape to know such a thing, he was oblivious to all that was going on around him at the moment, obsession had taken over and nothing else mattered.

"I want to see him now!" The voice cried out and suddenly the door was flung open.

Sheriff Russell was startled and almost fell backwards off his chair, standing in the doorway was a girl, wearing a massive yellow parka, and thick glasses, her mop of black curls homed a mass of snowflakes that were melting quickly, quite possibly from the heat of her glowing face. It was a face of annoyance, verging on anger and it was focused straight at Sheriff Russell.

"Is this him?" She spat with derision, her face creased as if unimpressed by the sight that met her eyes.

"What is going on?" Sheriff Russell asked.
Lieutenant Adams grabbed her by the shoulder and tried to remove her.

"I'm sorry Sheriff, she refused to listen..." Adams began but was interrupted by the girl who tore herself away from the Lieutenant's grip.

"Get your hands off me!" She growled, "I know my rights!"

"Now you listen here..." Adams growled back.

"Tammy, it's okay." Sheriff Russell sighed, rubbing vigorously at his temples.

"But..." Adams tried again to speak, but her voice was too loud and her tone seemed to pierce through his brain like an ice pick.

"Just tell me what's going on." The Sheriff said, "Who is this young lady and what does she want?"

"She is…" Adams again failed in finishing a full sentence.

"Agnes!" The girl beat the Lieutenant to it, "Agnes Duckworth."

"Duckworth?" Sheriff Russell murmured, searching the back of his mind as though the name was ringing a bell in his memory.

"Yeah, my brother went missing out here last year and I'm here to find out what the fuck you are doing about it?"

"Hey!" Adams cried, "There's no need for that kind of…"

"Tammy, Tammy," The Sheriff grimaced at the loudness, "it's okay. Leave us alone for a while, let Miss Duckworth say what she has to say."

"But Sheriff…"

"Please?" He smiled, it was the look he used to give her, for a split second the old Patrick Russell had returned and she couldn't resist that look, she melted and smiled.

"Would you like a coffee?" Adams asked, more to the Sheriff than to Agnes, but Agnes answered anyway.

"No! I want answers, not coffee."

"Black please." Russell nodded and he smiled as Tammy closed the door and left the two alone.

"So what have you been doing about it, huh?" Agnes snapped and folded her arms.

"Please sit down." Sheriff Russell asked gently, gesturing to the seat at the other side of the desk.

"I don't want to sit down, I want to..."

"SIT!" He growled.

Agnes' eyes widened and she succumbed and sat down with a defiant thud, arms still crossed over her chest.

"So, Agnes, your brother..."

"Yeah, Chester, where is he? What's happened to him? What are you doing about finding him?"

"Please calm down, I need to think." Russell seemed to be dazed by the flurry of words fired at him. Her eyes found the empty bottle of whiskey turned up in the wastepaper basket and she snarled at him.

"I see what you have been doing with your time! Drinking yourself to death when my brother is out there somewhere."

Russell couldn't take any more of her rabbiting and he snapped, slapping the desk and growling at her.

"YOUR BROTHER IS DEAD!"

Agnes sank back into her chair and wept, her hands rising up to cover her eyes that welled up underneath her spectacles.

Sheriff Russell rubbed at his temples again, wondering which hurt his head more, her shouting or her crying.

"I didn't mean...I shouldn't have..." Sheriff Russell said, scrambling for the right words, but he couldn't find them.

"How do you know?" Agnes snapped, tears magnified in the thick glass of her spectacles.

"I...I don't know for certain, but my gut tells me I'm unfortunately correct."

"Your gut? Your fucking gut!"

"Miss Duckworth please..."

"If you ask me, by the look of you and that stench!" Her nose crinkled up and creased at the aroma of sweat and liquor in the air, "The only thing your gut is good for is holding liquor!"

"I don't have time for this!" Sheriff Russell growled as he stood up and retrieved his heavily fur lined parka and his ushanka hat that hung on a hat stand in the corner of his office.

"He's not dead, he can't be, I won't believe it!" Agnes said, rising to meet him.

"Look, Miss Duckworth I can't help you, I've done all I can, believe me."

"Done all you can?" She laughed and shook her head in disbelief, "What have you done exactly? If my brother is dead, then where is his body? Show me some damn evidence and I will walk away."

Sheriff Russell stared at her with no words for a reply, he turned away and slipped on his parka.

"Don't turn away from me." Agnes said, grabbing his arm, he turned quickly with an anger in his eyes, which subsided as soon as he saw the young lady standing before him and he extinguished the heat that formed up around the collar of his shirt.

"I said, I can't help you." His words were soft and gentle, but they did not soothe her.

"You'll give me some closure on this matter or I will haunt you until the day you die, Sheriff."
He laughed nervously, but her face was stone.

"I'm serious, Sheriff. I've got nowhere to be and I'm not leaving this stinking town until I have the truth."
He put his hat on and headed out of the door.

"If I find the truth, I just might join you when you leave."
Sheriff Russell left and Agnes grabbed her backpack and gave chase calling after him for the truth of what happened to her brother, but her words were ignored as he left the office and stepped out into the soft falling snow, clambering into his 4x4 and driving away at speed, chained tyres shredding through the layer of snow on the ground.
Agnes stood in the reception and dropped her backpack on the floor and fell to her knees sobbing.

"He can't be dead, I won't believe it, he can't be!" She cried.

Lieutenant Adams arrived with the hot steaming black coffee in her hands and knelt next to her.

"Here, take this, it's hot and sweet." Lieutenant Adams said with a caring smile.

"Thank you." Agnes said quietly as she took the mug, and felt the heat emitting from it on the cold tips of her fingers.

"Sheriff has been through a tough time these past twelve months, sorry if his tone is a little brash."

"We've all been through shit. I just need to know the truth."

"He's trying his best and it's cost him, believe me." Lieutenant Adams sighed and helped Agnes to her feet.

"It's not good enough." Agnes growled.

Tammy Adams didn't have an answer to that, maybe he had done all he could, maybe he hadn't done enough, she didn't know for sure. All she knew is that the whole ordeal had changed him and not for the good.

"Do you have a place to stay?" The Lieutenant asked.

"No, not yet, I haven't had time..."

"You thought you were gonna walk in here and there would be answers for you, didn't you?"

Agnes turned to her with a tear rolling down a freckled cheek and her head dropped to focus on the heat rising from the coffee.

"If only life was that easy kid." Tammy sighed.
Agnes sighed and nodded.

"There's a little motel in Downtree, it's called The Fallen Maple. Do you know where it is?"
Agnes met her with a shake of the head and to Tammy she looked like a scared little girl and that natural instinct kicked in of wanting, no needing to help her. Tammy had never married or had children and that is something that devastated her. There was once a baby growing inside her but it was a different time, the baby didn't make it, neither did the relationship she was in. The complications saw that her womb would never hold another child.

She wrapped an arm around Agnes's shoulder's and walked her to the door.

Deputy Clegg had just stepped through the door with his lunch pail in his hand and a breakfast pastry hanging from his mouth, singing loudly. It took Agnes by surprise and she dropped the coffee to the linoleum below and it splashed up against Clegg's pants.

"Whoa!" Clegg complained.

"Raymond!"

Tammy shook her head and rolled her eyes at him.

"What did I do?" He groaned.

The Lieutenant walked past him, grabbing her parka that was slung over her chair at reception. She grabbed the mop that was leant up against the wall and thrust it into Clegg's hand, causing him to drop his lunch pail too.

"Raymond, get this mess cleaned up."

"I've only just walked through the door." Clegg complained, still chewing on the pastry.

"Tough!" Adams spat and led the girl out of the office, leaving Deputy Clegg standing in the middle of the empty reception area looking like a spare part.

"I'm supposed to be the Deputy here!" He called out loudly to no one, "I'm not the janitor!"
He sighed and chewed the remains of the pastry and started to swipe the mop over the puddle of coffee that was rapidly spreading out before him.
Sergeant Nathan Brown appeared from the locker room having just finished the night shift and smiled at Clegg.

"Hey Raymond! Congratulations, you finally got that promotion." He laughed and slapped Clegg on the back as he left the Deputy to grumble as he cleaned up the mess.

CHAPTER 5

The snow had slowed to a gentle flutter around Old Syrup, the chill had settled and any cracked or broken ice had frozen again during the night.

Sheriff Russell knelt on the ice where the remains of a broken ice shanty lay in pieces, covered with a layer of snow as if it had always been there. He pondered for a moment as he tried to understand what had taken place, but the best he could come up with was that some animal had mistaken it for prey in the snowstorm and ploughed into it, a grizzly or moose perhaps?

He stood up and heard his creaking joints echo around the frozen lake, he wiped away the snow that had settled on his knee and gazed around the scene. The ice shimmered in the cool morning air, although the sun couldn't be seen through the clouds that concealed it with greys and pinks, it was still bright and something on the ice caught his attention. The soles of his boots scraped across the ice as he made his way to this beacon. Lying on the ice, half covered in snow was a bent and twisted hand auger. He frowned and knelt again for a closer inspection, lifting the item up in his gloved hands and turning it around and around.

An old hand auger. Nobody has been ice fishing on The Syrup for more than twelve months. It could be that this had been left in the shanty by mistake.

He wiped away snow and noticed the fresh notches that had marked the shaft as if it had been hit by something heavy and sharp. As he investigated the tool further he noticed that there were some letters etched into its grip.

"E.P." He said to himself, the letters escaping his chapped lips in a plume of breath that took to the air.

"Elroy Pascoe!" He exclaimed.

There was a sound of rustling in the shrubs that surrounded the lake and his eyes grew wide. Flicking away the false snap on his holster he grasped the handle of his revolver. He stood up quickly and slipped on the ice almost tumbling into the broken remains of the shanty, but he managed to keep upright. If such a thing would have happened a few hours ago he would have no doubt hit the ice, but the fresh cold air had sobered him up.

He gazed around listening for the sound again but there seemed to be nothing, it took several moments to realise he was holding his breath and suddenly he exhaled, warm vapour dancing around him. As the cloud of breath cleared he saw something in a shrub and slowly walked across the ice towards it, but it was difficult to stop the scraping of his boots on the ice which echoed loudly around the trees and gave away his every movement. There was a rustle again and he slowly knelt and laid down the auger on the ice before unsheathing his weapon and holding it in both hands aimed and ready at the shrub. He seemed to hold his breath again but his heart was racing and beating rapidly in his chest as anticipation forced adrenaline around his body.

"Come on you fucker, come one." He murmured hoping and praying that it was the one he'd been searching for the last twelve months. That monster he believed to be responsible for all those missing people every winter. He quickly removed his gloves and readied his aim again, a clammy finger twitching on the trigger as his pulse thumped louder and louder uncontrollably in his ears, enough to drive a man insane.

"It's Beau Tooth." He seethed through gritted teeth, the name sounded like the hiss of a snake as it expanded into the cold breeze, "I just know it is. I just know it!"

The Sheriff was willing it to be the target so much that every muscle in his body seemed to tense at the same time and his index finger grew heavy, slightly pulling on the trigger until whatever was responsible stepped out from behind the shrub.

Patrick Russell was too far gone in his routine and fired, but at the last split second he managed to move the revolver away from the target and sent a bullet hurtling into the clouds above. The sound seemed to stay with him for the longest time as if the bullet was doing several laps of honour around Old Syrup.

His breaths were heavy and a layer of sweat fell from beneath the thick fur of his ushanka hat and he began to laugh as a wolverine stared at him, dark eyes wide with bewilderment, frozen to the spot by the fear of the loud sound.

"Go on you little bastard, get on out of here." He said.

The wolverine had seemed to be waiting for the words and scurried away into the cover of the trees.

The Sheriff holstered his gun and slipped his gloves back on before returning his focus to the hand auger. He picked it up and examined it again, before trudging off the lake and heading towards the bank.

"Is that where you were Elroy? Were you ice fishing when you disappeared?"

If he was waiting for a reply from Elroy Pascoe, he would be waiting a long time.

Sheriff Russell took this as a small win, it was the first clue he had found for over twelve months and if he could find the whereabouts of Elroy Pascoe from it, then at least that was something.

He walked away from the lake as snow fell again smothering other items that he may have seen if he had stayed around to investigate longer. A thermos, with the frozen remains of coffee still within. A pair of enamel mugs, a broken gas lamp and at closer inspection frozen droplets of blood clinging to the splintering wood that was once an ice shanty. He may have also noticed a circle in the ice, although the lake had frozen over again during the night, it was not as thick as the rest of the lake and a ring was noticeable, if you knew where to look for it. Shrubs moved again and heavy feet crunched in the snow watching as Sheriff Russell left the lake and headed back into town, this time it wasn't a wolverine that was watching.

CHAPTER 6

Dawn Rougeau shuffled around behind the counter of her diner almost in autopilot, each movement robotic in its nature as if her mind was on something else. The past twelve months had been considerably hard on her and it showed, she had lost a considerable amount of weight, not that she was overweight to start with, far from it, but the guilt that hung over her like a dark cloud had made her unable to keep most meals down. The bags under her eyes were heavy, showing visible signs that she was sleep deprived, but when the human mind is caught in a vice of guilt, sleep becomes near impossible.

The usual suspects sat at the counter and enjoyed late breakfasts of bacon and pancakes slathered with maple syrup. That was one thing that hadn't changed at *Dawn's*, the food was still up to scratch, in fact the daily routine of feeding these hungry bellies was the only thing that had kept her going.

Dawn had had some awful thoughts, a voice screamed at her on a daily basis to end her life, that she was not worthy to breathe that ice cold air that surrounded her within the snow globe of Maple Falls. She knew that what she had done or what her actions had allowed to happen were wrong, the guilt that she wore now was like a jacket made from cement. There was no getting away from the fact that she had led those kids to their deaths and just the thought of them in the grip of that monster made her feel sick. Those awful thoughts came quite often but she believed she was too much of a coward to go through with it, to take her own life was seen as a way out for some, but for her she believed that what she had done would surely mean there was a place waiting for her in hell, where her guilt would no doubt be chained to her for eternity.

She shook away the horrendous thoughts of suicide and tried to focus on her customers, a smile fixed by lipstick helped her appear more welcoming than she felt. But she had to wear the mask of a pleasant waitress or she would no doubt see her diner empty of custom.

Who wants to eat their breakfast with the reaper gazing over at them?

Dawn wiped at the counter with a damp cloth, she had been wiping the same spot now for the past twenty minutes until the voice of one of her most loyal customers brought her out of her revery.

"I think you got it Dawn." Cackled the toothless maw of Jeff Thurman, or Old Sparky to his friends.

"Huh?" Dawn replied and gazed through him.

"You've been cleaning that same spot for a while now. I think it's clean."

"Sorry, Sparky." She sighed, "I was miles away." Old Sparky didn't reply with words but with a nod of his head and returned to eating his bacon, which was no easy feat with so little teeth.

He didn't have to reply, he knew what she had gone through, what the whole town had been going through each winter, he didn't need to say a word.

"Quiet in here today." Dawn said gazing out at the tables and booths that stood idle, only Old Sparky and two other aging gentlemen sat at the counter.

"Yeah, looks like Abe and Howie didn't make it in today."

"Wonder what those pair of scallywags have been up to?" Dawn smiled, the action seemed almost alien to her these days and seemed to crack the red lipstick of her mask.

"Probably drunk." Sniffed Sparky.

The door clattered when it opened, bringing in the breeze and the sound of the chilling wind and Dawn turned, certain that it would be Abe Slapawitz or Howie Kendal. She was taken aback in surprise as a young woman stood in the doorway. Her mass of black curls in disarray and flecked with melting snowflakes, her spectacles steamed up. She was wrapped in her large yellow parka and dithered against the cold.

"Come in my dear, come in!" Dawn exclaimed pleasantly, "You'll catch your death out there."

Old Sparky scoffed to himself, knowing just how true those words actually were, but Dawn ignored him and left her safe place behind the counter to approach the stranger and welcome her inside.

"Hi." Agnes said meekly, almost blushing.

As Dawn approached her, her mind played a cruel trick on her eyes and for a split second she saw the girl that arrived with her friends last year standing in front of her and it caused her to slow her pace and shudder. A queasy feeling knotted her stomach and this must have shown on her face.

"Is something wrong?" Agnes asked.

Dawn shook her head and with the action the vision disappeared.

"Oh, nothing." Dawn replied with a smile, "You just reminded me of someone that's all. Now what can I do for you?"

"I'm staying at the Fallen Maple Motel, but they don't do breakfast and I'm starving. I haven't eaten since last night."

"Well, we will have to do something about that shan't we?" Dawn smiled, it felt so good to genuinely smile again.

She wrapped her arm around Agnes and led her to a booth in the corner.

"I'll put you in this booth. It's furthest from the door and closest to the heater." Dawn winked.

"Thanks." Agnes grinned and sat, unzipping her parka, but not yet warm enough to remove it. Underneath she wore an orange hoodie with Haast University printed on it in faded black print.

"Besides you don't want to sit next to those old codgers now do you?" She whispered and winked again.

"I heard that." Bellowed Old Sparky, "I might be as old as God's dog, but there ain't nothing wrong with my ears."

Dawn and Agnes sniggered.

"Now what could I get ya on this first day of winter?"

"I could really go for some of those pancakes and some syrup." Agnes said, eyeing the food up on a customer's plates, her mouth watering so much she had to lick away the saliva that was threatening to spill from her plump lips.

"You sure can." Dawn replied, "Anything to drink?"

"Could I get a tea?"

"Yep."

"Do you have Earl Grey by any chance?"

48

"We sure do." Dawn smiled, "Heaps in fact! None of these uncultured swines drink anything but coffee."

"Okay." Agnes smiled.

Dawn stood looking at her for a moment, praying that this one wouldn't fall to the same fate as those visitors did last winter.

"Is it really the first day of winter?" Agnes asked.

"Proper winter, yes." Dawn replied.

"What is proper winter?" Agnes asked.

"When the Tear Drop River freezes over." Old Sparky barked, "Then winter's here. Anything before that may as well be summer."

Dawn rolled her eyes at Old Sparky and Agnes giggled as Dawn returned to the counter.

Agnes slipped out a map of Maple Falls that she had got from the motel and started to study it as Dawn prepared her order.

Agnes investigated the map, her index finger hovering over the vast Maple Woods before settling on the location that read 'Lumberjack's Cabins'.

"Does anybody know how long it would take to get to the Lumberjack's Cabins?"

There was a sudden sound of smashing crockery as Agnes's breakfast left Dawn's shaking hand and hit the

49

floor. Old Sparky looked up from his bacon and gave Dawn a subtle shake of the head.

Dawn looked like a fawn in headlights, one that was so close to the oncoming truck that she could feel the heat exuding from its engine. Dawn's face was drawn and grey as she stood there gazing into space until Old Sparky gave a gruff cough.

The smile spread across her face again as if it had been spread on by a butterknife.

"Oops!" She exclaimed, "How clumsy of me. You may have to wait a while longer for your breakfast, honey."

"That's okay." Agnes said as she watched Dawn disappear behind the counter to clear up the mess.

"Must be my arthritis playing up again." Dawn laughed, but it wasn't convincing, "It plays the devil with my grip. Especially this time of year."

"So, what about these cabins?" Agnes said appearing next to Sparky and making him jump and almost choke on a rasher of bacon he was sucking the syrup off.

Agnes slapped him on the back.

"Easy there old timer." She said with a chuckle.

Old Sparky glared at her and grumbled something that was incomprehensible, causing Agnes to shrug and lean over the counter to witness Dawn scooping up the remains of the broken plate.

"So the Lumberjack's Cabins?" Agnes asked again, "Do you know how to get there?"

"I...I...can't say that I do, honey. Sorry." Dawn said standing and sliding the contents of her dustpan into the trash without making eye contact with the girl.

"Oh, that's odd." Agnes said, looking at her with a hint of suspicion that wrinkled her brow.

"Oh, how so?" Dawn asked, still unable to meet Agnes's stare as she swept a mop around the floor, the damp head sliding in the spilt puddle of maple syrup.

"Well, you own them don't you?" Agnes said matter-of-factly.

Dawn could not reply, or even face her now as she moved back over to where her bucket was stationed and slipped the dirty mop back into the disinfected water.

"You are Dawn Rougeau aren't you? And you own the Lumberjack's Cabins that you let out online."

"Well...I...I..." Dawn stuttered gazing at Old Sparky for some assistance but there was none forthcoming.

"You let it out last winter to my brother and his friends..." Agnes's eyes filled up and her cheeks became flush, she knew that Dawn was hiding something and she had no time for such games. "...he never came home. Neither did his friends."

"Oh that's a shame. Perhaps they ran away, people run away from home all the time." Dawn grimaced, knowing it was a stupid thing to say, before she finally looked at Agnes who seemed distressed. Dawn's eyes softened with pity for the girl and shame for herself as she watched Agnes collapse onto the stool next to Old Sparky at the counter. He stood up grumbling and took his breakfast to a quiet part of the diner.

"I just want to find my brother." She sobbed and Dawn approached and put a hand on hers and patted it gently.

"Your hands are freezing!" Dawn gasped and quickly poured her that earl grey tea that she had been waiting for.

"Here."

"Thanks." Agnes said with an embarrassed smile, she slipped her hands around the mug and didn't even drink any, for the moment she was happy to just enjoy its warmth.

"I do know where the cabins are." Dawn said with a sigh as she walked around the counter and perched on a stool next to Agnes.

"So you own them?"

Dawn nodded, a look of sheepishness swept across her face and her eyes met the worn toe-ends of her once white dockside shoes.

"And you let out the cabins to my brother? His name was Duckworth. Chester Duckworth. He was with six others..."

"Yes." Dawn interrupted her, "Yes I did."

"Then why did you act like you didn't know anything about the cabins?" Agnes interrogated.

"I...I'm sorry, but...it's difficult for me to talk about it."

"Talk about what?" Agnes said standing and grabbing Dawn by her shoulders and shaking her, "About what damn it! If you know something you have to tell me."

She shook her aggressively, not meaning to hurt her, but she was consumed by the desperation and anger that she felt.

"What happened to my brother?!" She cried and Dawn sobbed into her hands.

"That is enough!" Said a voice of authority.

All eyes turned to the entrance of the diner and Sheriff Russell stood there with a face as stern and as hard as granite.

"I..." Agnes said and realised that she was gripping Dawn way too tight and she let go of her immediately, "I'm sorry, I didn't mean to hurt you."

"It's okay, it's okay." Dawn sniffed, "It's only what I deserve."

"What do you mean by that?" Agnes asked again, a dozen questions racing through her head.

"Dawn!" Snapped Sheriff Russell and that was enough to send her running to the back area sobbing.

"What did she mean? Won't somebody tell me what the hell is going on in this fucking place?"

"I said that's enough. Now leave." The Sheriff said and pointed to the door.

"But..."

"But nothing. Get out!" Sheriff Russell had a bite to his tone, but there was a sadness in his eyes and Agnes seemed to pick up on this, but not wanting to push her luck and spend the night in a cold cell she decided to go along with the Sheriff's wishes.

"Fine." Agnes sighed and returned to the booth where she retrieved her map.

Sheriff Russell trailed Dawn as Agnes watched through the back room's circular window cut into the door. The Sheriff hugged her and rubbed at her back as she wiped away tears with a handkerchief.

Old Sparky appeared at her side and whispered quietly to her.

"If you knew what was good for ya, you'd stay away from those cabins."

"Why?"

"You wanna die young?"

"No. No, of course not."

54

"Then heed an old man's warning and leave it well alone."

Old Sparky returned to his original seat at the counter and Agnes looked around at the diner, it would appear there was nothing more she could learn from being here. Sheriff Russell appeared behind the counter and placed his hands on his hips and Agnes zipped up her parka and left the diner.

CHAPTER 7

The Lumberjack's Cabins sat quietly, without a groan or creak, perhaps for fear of what stalked the woods of Maple Falls when the snow started to fall. The cabins stood dotted around the area, each one sunken in a shallow grave of snow and ice, although they had been left on purpose, forgotten with the hope that they would fester and rot. Maple Falls prayed that the snow would drag the constructions deep down beneath the surface, out of sight and out of mind. The people of Maple Falls hoped they could forget about the atrocities that were committed there, each winter a hope that the heavy burden of snow would do its job and conceal them from the world.

Snow covered the roofs of the cabins and deep drifts swept from the wooden walls, but still the cabins refused to be taken completely.

It was incredible how silent the woods seemed to be when the snow fell, it was as if Mother Nature paused from her routine, silencing the wildlife and quelling the whistle of the wind and the flicker of branches to take in such a surreal, chilling fantasia.

The sweet sound of nothingness was soon disrupted by the heavy trudging sound of footfalls crunching through the snow. All at once the wind returned, whistling a warning to whoever may be too near to this approaching bane. Flee, scratched the branches as the whispering warning from the wind caressed them. Words of warning from the surrounding woods that were never heard by those it intended to counsel. The wildlife heeded the warnings, they knew the signs, smelt the retching aroma of rotting flesh and dried blood and heard the familiar sounds of scraping chains and of an axe cutting through the sharp winter air.

Beau Tooth entered the site and gazed with some kind of pleasant reverie that pricked at his subconscious. Some memory from the past that tugged at his emotions, an emotion that he was almost completely void of, happiness. His black heart seemed to skip an unfamiliar rhythm for a moment as his mismatched eyes stared at one cabin in particular. Somewhere deep inside him was the echo of children's laughter, but it was smothered immediately, it was in the past now, forgotten and inside the laughter turned to screams, that made him smile. A wriggling worm of sadism moved across his scarred face, a smile like no other, a cleft palette helped to contort the curve of chapped and split skin around his lips into something sinister. The freezing snow seemed to nip at the exposed flesh of his massive forearms, flesh almost black in places from the biting frost and ice, but he showed no indication of discomfort or pain. With his clothes tattered and torn it was seemingly impossible that anyone could survive these conditions, but somehow Beau Tooth did.

He stepped closer to the sleeping cabins shuffling into the deeper snow that was already meeting his knee caps, he knew all too well that in a few days time it could be up to his neck and then hunting became more problematic. Tooth knew that if he could retrieve enough game in the first few days of winter then he would be quite content for another twelve months living in the wilderness.

Something made him halt and gaze around the area, his brow furrowed with confusion as if some pawns were missing from the board.

How could he play his game without the right pieces in place?

There were no vehicles parked around the area, no tracks in the snow from man or machine. The cabins sat in darkness and although it was midday, there would usually still be some lights illuminating the gloom of the area. The stone built chimneys that sprouted from each roof sat idle too without the hot, bellowing plumes of smoke signalling that anyone was there. Beau Tooth growled and cracked frostbitten fingers that creaked like old worn leather as he clenched them tightly in anger.

He realised that he was alone.

The anger spurred him forward and he drove through the deepening snow quickly, cutting through it like a human snow plough and attacked the cabin in front of him. There was still police tape pinned to the door and it flapped around him as he smashed through it, the tape seemed to grope and cling to him in some feeble attempt to stop his progress. He strode across the warped floorboards that seemed to protest with each cumbersome stride until he stopped in the centre of the cabin. There was nothing, the living area still smelt of stale blood and death, it was a familiar scent that caressed his nostrils, but the cabin itself was barren. These were the scents of an old hunt and all that remained was the screams in his head of those that were taken last hunting season. He growled and howled like some beast before turning over a table and using his axe to attack the furniture.

He stomped around the cabin at speed, driving his axe into anything and everything until he stopped, breaths heavy, massive chest rising and falling, a mask of disgust as his crooked teeth scraped together and saliva dribbled from his bulbous lips into his nest of a beard that still homed flecks of fresh snow.

Angrily he left and strode out into the snow to gaze around at the other cabins, all of them identical with barren lifelessness. He gazed up at the greying sky and allowed the snow to fall upon his face, the flakes seemed to seep into the contours of his scarred flesh, but they did nothing to cleanse the heat that caused his hairless head to glow with anger.

He let out a painful war cry of oppression, there had been no lambs led to slaughter this year and Beau Tooth knew what that meant. He clasped the axe in both hands wringing the worn wooden shaft and stomped away from the cabins, there was no game to be played here.

CHAPTER 8

With another day coming to an end in Maple Falls, the majority headed to *Chopper's* bar for a well earned beverage. Some drank to discuss the affairs of the day and put their graft at the back of their minds. Some drank to be social, to escape the shackles of living alone and being tied to the sofa watching old reruns on television. Others drank to forget and there was a lot that needed to be forgotten in this town.

Sheriff Russell was one of those that couldn't forget, he would not allow it, but he drank (some would say too much lately), drank to block it all out and help him sleep. Trouble was it took an awful lot to bring on the sleep and the effects had started to show, seeping through the cracks and tearing the life he once knew apart like unfixable shards of fabric.

When he entered *Chopper's,* immediately all eyes fell upon him. Some of those eyes were courteous and friendly, but behind those empathetic lids there were always the idle whispers of gossip and hearsay.

Unfortunately Patrick Russell lived his life in the view of the whole community and there was nothing he could do or say that wouldn't be observed by the prying population of Maple Falls. To them the Sheriff was theirs, public property and they believed he should serve no other purpose than to be at their beck and call every second of the ticking clock.

How dare he have a life of his own away from the badge.

The jukebox spluttered out an old *Sinatra* number, the one about the exchanging of glances between those strangers meeting in the night.

He smirked and chuckled to himself how apt the song was, for that is exactly how he felt, like a stranger to these people that he was trying his utmost to keep alive and safe.

Even the massive bulk of the trophy bear, Bigelow seemed to judge him as he entered, as did the marble-like eyes of the mounted heads of stags upon the walls. Eyes judging him, antlers pointing towards him with crooked accusations.

"Evening all." The Sheriff said, some of them grumbled in response as he made his way towards the bar.

One particular table acknowledged him with glares of bitterness, bitterness that was made worse when it had been fuelled by alcohol. A group of four burly men sat around a table. Each one of them with playing cards fanned out in their clammy digits as a plethora of empty bottles of Bobby's and dollar bills filled the centre of the table.

"Sheriff." Scoffed the biggest of them all, a barrel chested man with a thick black beard and greasy long hair. He chewed on a toothpick, his mouth contorting into a snarl more than a smile. The other men just glared at the Sheriff as he passed by.

"Ike." Came The Sheriff's reply, but he ignored the snarl and the glances that meant trouble.

"Rough day?" Ike sniggered, those around the table followed suit, "Being the first day of winter and all, I thought you might be out with your holy water and crucifix trying to nab that pesky ghoul that haunts the woods."

The Sheriff sighed and turned to him with a fire burning in his eyes, but he said nothing just stared into those eyes that matched his own, Ike Rayburn was just itching for a tussle.

"Yeah, Sheriff, some kind of ghoul-buster now, are ya?" Cackled Hank Jessop who sat next to Ike and prodded the Sheriff in his hip with the point of an elbow. The Sheriff shot him a look too but Hank playfully winked back and licked away beer foam that had built up on his thick hazel moustache.

"It's ghost-buster, Hank." Said Ira Berquist rolling his eyes and focusing his attention on his hand of cards, more than the confrontation that was taking place.

"Huh?" Grunted Hank, "What are you talking about Ira?"

"Yeah, pretty sure it's ghost-buster and not ghoul-buster." Agreed Ira's younger brother Ben who held his cards in one hand while whirling a bowie knife around his fingers expertly like some act from the circus.

The Sheriff eyed this action, the blade dancing on his fingertips masterfully, he wondered whether this routine was for him. A part of Sheriff Russell wished that Ben Berquist would grip that handle of the knife and make a plunge for him, any reason to make an example of these morons. Another voice inside his head wished for Ben Berquist to take the blade and swipe it across his throat and be done with it all or better still hand him the knife and he'd do it himself.

"Oh shit, Ben, does it really fucking matter?" Hank grumbled.

"Yeah, ghouls and ghosts." Ben grinned, "It's all the same isn't it, Sheriff."

Russell's eyes made it back to Ben's and his fists clenched so very tightly. Ben must have seen the gesture and spread his wide body out in his seat, allowing his legs to stretch out in front of the Sheriff and slowly crossing them creating a barrier at his feet.

"Careful now Sheriff." Ben said with a smile.

Sheriff Russell said nothing, but his eyes burned in a frenzy.

"Yeah, careful." Hank echoed Ben and moved in his seat, allowing his revolver he wore on his belt to be seen.

"You got a permit for that peashooter, Hank?" Sheriff asked.

Hank laughed and tapped the handle of the revolver.

"I seem to have misplaced it, Sheriff." Hank grinned.

"Maybe it's outside, Hank." Ike growled through a false smile of craggy teeth, "Maybe the good old Sheriff here wants to go outside and help you look for it?"

"You boys hold on, I need to have a drink first." Sheriff Russell said as he stepped over the outstretched legs of Ben Berquist who chuckled to himself.

"You'll need more than a drink, Sheriff." Ira said under his breath but just loud enough for him to hear, the words or sentiment didn't phase him as he continued away from the table and they erupted into laughter before returning to their game.

In that laughter Sheriff Russell heard a thousand taunts and it halted him, none of the men at the table saw this, none of them saw him turn around and ball his fists again.

"Patrick." Came a friendly croak, like a heavy boot on gravel and it was enough to make him see sense and he turned towards the bar to see the proprietors of the establishment standing behind it.

"That'll do." Came the voice again, the voice of Chopper Hardwood, wringing at a damp towel and looking at him with disappointment, the way a father might look at a wayward son.

"Come on now, Sheriff, it's not worth the effort." Said Chopper's wife Wendy, who smiled and slapped a hand on the bar at the place he always sat. He turned back towards the bar and grinned, sheepishly, before approaching them and collapsing onto his favourite stool.

"Now, what was all that about?" Chopper asked.

"Oh, nothing." Sheriff Russell sighed as he removed his ushanka, placed it on the bar and scratched at his greasy hairline.

"You better not be trying to start a ruckus in my bar." Chopper said playfully.

"I wouldn't dream of it, Chopper." Sheriff Russell exclaimed, holding his hands aloft.

"Good to hear it." Chopper sniffed as he whipped the damp towel towards the Sheriff, making him flinch.

"Knock it off you two." Wendy sighed, slapping Chopper on his back before walking away to see to a gaggle of customers that surrounded the other end of the bar.

"The usual?" Chopper asked, already knowing the answer and disappearing under the bar to retrieve the bottle of Hackenschmidt whiskey that would no doubt soon be empty.

"Of course." Sheriff Russell said with boyish eagerness.

"You've been giving this a right pounding of late, Patrick. Maybe you should take it easy for a while." Chopper said as he poured them both a glass.

"I will." Said the Sheriff, but then immediately downed the aging whiskey, while Chopper sipped at his.

"Christ, Patrick!" Chopper exclaimed, "I said take it easy."

"I'll take another, Chopper." He said, ignoring the bartender's words and sliding the glass back towards him.

Chopper looked at him and the glass indecisively for a moment and then over at his wife who was standing looking at him from the other end of the bar shaking her head.

"Patrick..."

"C'mon Chopper." He pleaded, "You know what to do."

Chopper gave in with a sigh and poured him another hefty serving, much to the displeasure of his wife, who threw her arms into the air and turned her back on the situation.

The Sheriff grabbed the glass and attempted to down it but Chopper trapped his wrist and halted the proceedings.

"I said take it easy." Chopper whispered, the tone was strong, but the words were said with care.

"What do you think you are doing?" The Sheriff said, a little rattled, his cheeks glowing with annoyance.

"Looking out for a dear friend." Came Chopper's answer and the words were enough to calm the Sheriff down, he replied with a nod and lowered the glass back down. The whiskey seemed to call to him like some alluring mistress, forcing him to lick at his lips, but this time he was able to ignore her advances.

"You look like shit." Chopper said matter-of-factly as he took another sip from his own glass.

"Say it like it is." Russell chuckled.

"I mean c'mon kid. This ain't you, look at yourself."

"Oh, but it is me, Chopper. It's very much me."

He sighed heavily and took a small sip of the whiskey he had been craving for, it burnt his throat on the way down, it wasn't an unpleasant sensation, more of a familiar one.

"I know you have been through a lot these last twelve months, but you have to slow down, professionally and socially!" He eyed the bottle on the bar, before seizing it and sliding it back under the counter.

"'Been through a lot'! That's the understatement of the year." Russell scoffed and took another sip.

"Well, you have." Chopper sighed, "I don't know what I can say to you anymore. It has to stop."

"What, drinking?" Russell exclaimed and then laughed, "What kind of business are you trying to run here? I never heard of a landlord telling his customers not to drink."

"Seriously." Chopper said, with a caring hand on the Sheriff's arm.

"Easy now, Chopper." Russell smiled, "You'll be having your regulars thinking there is something going on between you and I."

Russell laughed again and blew a kiss at the bartender.

"Idiot!" Chopper grumbled as he whipped his hand away.

"Don't give those dipshits more ammunition to fire at me."

"It's not just the drink though is it? It's not even Holly leaving is it?"

69

"Leave it Chopper."

"But…"

"I said leave it!" He growled, he sighed immediately, he could never stay mad at Chopper, even if he wanted to, "Just drop it. I don't want to talk about her."

"Then what about…"

"Here we go again." He sighed and rolled his eyes before taking another sip.

"This search for 'you know who', it's becoming an obsession."

"'You know who'? Jesus Christ Chopper! My friend, we are well past that! We are well past using code names for that bastard. Use his fucking name."
"No…I can't."

"I can Beau…Tooth!" Russell grinned a drunken grin, "Everybody knows Chopper. You're the only one trying to keep it a secret. And what's the point of a secret if everybody already knows the truth? Who are you trying to keep it from? Yourself? Are you trying to delude yourself of his existence now? If I remember correctly it was you that told me about him in the first place!" Russell said before taking another sip, most of it dribbled down his chin as he hurried to speak again.

"I should probably blame you for all of it, if you hadn't told me about him I would have been none the wiser and would have been just as oblivious as everybody else seems to be in this fucking town!"

"That's enough, Patrick." Chopper seethed, "I told you about him because I thought you needed to know. I thought you could be the one to put a stop to it all."

"Yeah, well, how did that work out for ya?"

"You're right, it is my fault. I should have never said anything."

"Shall I just forget that you told me then? Is that it? Move on with my life and just let innocent people continue to be hauled off by this bastard. Is that what you want me to do?"

"No, but..."

"FUCK IT!" He declared holding his hands aloft and standing up from his stool, "Beau Tooth is real! I'm going to catch him and hang him up in the centre of town for you all to see!"

There was laughter from Ira and his followers at the card table and they took obvious pleasure by hollering obscenities towards him.

"Will you sit yourself down!" Wendy seethed slamming her hands down on the bar.

"Sorry Wendy." Russell said with a glow of embarrassment as he collapsed back onto the stool.

71

"You're showing yourself up, Sheriff." Wendy said before turning to Chopper, "What did you say to him to get him all fired up?"

"Nothing!" Chopper denied.

"He was telling me to forget about Beau Tooth again." Russell slumped on the bar sipping his whiskey.

"What have I told you about mentioning him?" Wendy growled at her husband and slapped him on the back again.

"If this is what married life becomes, I'm glad my wife left me." Russell sniggered.

Wendy sighed and strutted away from them.

"Who's Beau Tooth?" A voice came from behind the Sheriff and he turned in his seat to be faced by Agnes.

"Oh God! Not you again!" Russell grumbled and collapsed onto the bar in a heap.

"What can I get you, miss?" Chopper asked.

"I don't want a drink, I just want information that's all."

"Information about what?" Chopper said, his eyes squinting with suspicion.

"About what happened to my brother out in those woods last year." Agnes said, sitting on the stool next to the Sheriff.

He groaned and his face creased up at her.

"Why won't you just leave me alone?" Russell asked.

"Maybe I don't need you, maybe Mister Chopper will tell me with all I need to know."

"I don't know nothing, Miss." Chopper replied and started to wipe the bar with his towel.

"Lots of people in this town and they all seem to know nothing." Agnes scoffed.

"I don't know what to tell ya." Chopper shrugged.

"What about this Beau Tooth character? Who is he? What was the Sheriff yelling about?"

"Pay him no mind, he's drunk that's all. Talking nonsense."

"As usual." Laughed Russell as he took another sip.

"Somebody needs to start telling me something and it needs to be the truth or I'll be going into that wood myself and..."

"NO!" Sheriff Russell, Chopper and Wendy all cried out at the same time and caused her to stumble backwards off her stool and step away from them.

"There is something in those woods isn't there?" She said, "This Beau Tooth character?"

"No, honey, he's just an...an urban legend that's all, just a boogeyman that they tell the kids about to

73

keep them out of the woods, that's all." Wendy said with a smile that was caring, but unconvincing.

"All woods are dangerous, Miss. Bears and cougars and what not, that's why we're telling you to stay out of them, nothing more."

"I don't buy it." Agnes scoffed.

"Good! Cause it's not for sale." Sheriff Russell laughed and he staggered from the stool and took the last of his whiskey down in one gulp.

"Are you going to help me find my brother?" Agnes asked him as he swayed from side to side.

"Well, are you? Or have I got to seek out this Beau Tooth myself?"

Sheriff Russell tried to open his eyes wide to focus on her, but he saw multiple figures standing in front of him, all of them Agnes Duckworth, all of them quivering in front of him.

"Your brother is dead..." Russell said before collapsing to the floor in an unconscious sleep at Agnes's feet.

CHAPTER 9

The wailing cry of a banshee echoed through the woods, it was a horrendous sound that was enough to send a shiver down the spines of even the bravest individual.

Edward Gotch had heard many strange sounds seep out from the woods, especially in the dead of night and especially in the winter. Edward had sat for the last few hours in his cracked and worn leather armchair, gripping his rifle. The sound was like nothing he had ever experienced before, it seemed that each time the yowl met his ears that it shook the walls and roof of his makeshift shack. His eyes were old and as dark as chestnuts and although they were wise, they were scared. The snow and the wind did not help matters, the wind constantly looked for weaknesses in the shack and burrowed inside to send a chill down his spine. He had tried to fix the holes, every fall he would try, but he always seemed to miss some and that bitter wind always found a way in.

His candles flickered, he had no electricity, but for a small generator and gas for the lamps was getting expensive to buy, cheap as he was he stuck to candles.

His sheepdog didn't like the queer sound either and whined as she curled herself around his feet.

"Hush now Nora, it's okay." Edward said in a reassuring tone as he reached down and stroked her, he didn't believe the words himself, so how was he meant to convince her?

The sound seemed to have grown closer still, with each howl of wind and flurry of snow that hit his window, it grew nearer.

"Must be some animal, sounds wounded." Edward announced, nodding along with the words trying to believe them.

He had spent the afternoon clearing the corrugated roof of the excess snow and shovelling a pathway to the road known as Maple Cross. He had lived there for many years now on the corner of the crossroads that led to Maple Drive, Maple Falls and the tiny town of Dekker. He had heard all the stories and never truly believed them, he believed what his eyes saw and he had never seen anything.

"Yeah, that's what it will be, I'll bet. Some wounded...animal."

But for the life of him he didn't know what type of creature would make such a heinous cry.

"Perhaps I should go and see?" He asked nobody in particular. If he was asking for Nora's advice the answer was most definitely 'no', as she shuffled underneath the armchair and whined some more.

"Oh, c'mon now Nora, if I gotta be brave you have to be brave too."

Edward stood up from the armchair and shuffled to the window where he peered out into the white wilderness.

"At least it's stopped snowing, at least that's one good thing."

Nora's sad eyes gazed up at him and grumbled.

"It'll be okay." He smiled at her, "I've got my gun. We will just go and have a look and if we see something out of the ordinary, we'll come straight back in and call the Sheriff's office on the good old citizen band."

Edward gazed over at the old citizen band transceiver that he had been given many years ago by former Sheriff, Keith W. Windwood. It had been gifted to him in case anything out of the ordinary happened in the woods. Edward had not known what Windwood had meant by that but he kept it anyway, not that he had ever had to use it. It just sat there gathering dust next to his portable television with its ridiculously long aerial protruding from it, constantly straining to get a signal. The screen was currently playing a rerun of *Gilligan's Island* with a stripe of snow scuttling across the screen accompanied by the scratching sound of white noise.

"Then we can have a bit of chow and watch Magnum Pa, how's that sound?"

Nora shuffled out from underneath the armchair, she was a sucker for *Tom Selleck*, so she joined him at his side as he slipped on his old parka, navy blue with a fur hood, it had seen better days and was ripped in places now, the worse holes had been fixed with duct tape.

"There's a brave girl." He smiled and patted her as he clutched the rifle in his hand and opened the door. He snatched up a flashlight and flicked the switch just to make sure it was working, it was and he turned it off again.

The hinges shrieked, it was the sound his old bones would have made against the bitterness of the conditions, if they could talk that was. The wind ruffled Nora's grey, black coat and sent her retreating slowly back to the safety of the armchair.

"C'mon now, Nora, don't be like that girl."

She whined and climbed up on the seat of the armchair and curled up.

"Fine, have it your way, but if I'm attacked by some rabid raccoon then it's on your head!"

Edward Gotch stepped out into the snow and closed the door behind him, he stood gripping the rifle and listened. The wind brought with it the northern chill and flakes of ice that it had dislodged from the massive pine trees that rose into the clouds.

Edward gripped the gun tightly and shuffled out into the edge of the woods that surrounded his little shack. He heard nothing but the wind for a time and as he grew braver he stepped into the woods. Then in a clearing he heard the sound again, that harpy's cry that sounded as if it had been conjured up by hell itself.

"What is that?" He murmured, shivering more from the sound than the weather.

As the wind blew stronger, joining this wailing croak of pain, he believed he heard the words 'Help me'.

"It can't be?" He gasped, "Is there someone out there?" He called, but still was met by the relentless cry.

"HELLO?" He cried at the top of his voice and all at once the sound stopped, replaced by the silence of the woods. There was nothing, it was as if the wind had stopped blowing too.

"Is someone there? Is someone hurt?" Edward called again but was met by no reply.

He trudged forward, closer to the clearing where there was a large mound of snow, he believed that this was where the sound was coming from, he switched on the flashlight and it lit the gloom as well as one could when the surroundings were mostly white.

"I can help you if need be?"

As he closed in on the mound he realised it was an old sledge and whatever it was carrying was covered in a layer of snow.

Edward believed that maybe the horse pulling the sledge had possibly bolted and that the owner may have fallen and was hurt. As he approached he saw movement on the other side of the sledge.

"Don't be afraid, I can help. I can offer you a hot cup of Joe, would you like that? Warm you up a little?"

Whatever seemed to move on the other side of the sledge had gone when he got there.

Edward's brow furrowed and he gazed around into the deepness of the woods that were becoming darker with every passing moment, night was drawing in and he didn't want to be out in it.

"Hello?" He called again, he would not be able to live with himself if there was someone out here hurt and he did nothing about it.

"Are you there?"

Nothing.

He turned his attention to the sledge and stared with bewilderment at the strange shapes that were contorted in a pile on the back of the old sledge, covered in a blanket of snow. He could have sworn that he saw something staring back at him, glistening in the shard of light that exploded from his flashlight. He reached forwards and wiped away the snow to reveal the frozen face of Howie Kendal, the burnt flesh and petrified expression preserved for eternity.

"Good God!" Edward gasped backing away from the sledge and realising that there were two frozen dead bodies sat upon it. He staggered backwards and into something that he believed was the trunk of a tree but that was too much to hope for. As he turned he came face to face with Beau Tooth, the flashlight illuminating every sordid crease and scar on his haggard face. Edward let out a croaking scream and staggered away from the gargantuan beast of a man who just smiled at him sadistically.

"I-I don't want no trouble now, okay big fella. You j-just go about your business." He stuttered as he stepped away, edging back the way he had come, when Beau Tooth revealed his hefty axe and cradled it in his chapped, frost bitten hands he had seen enough.

"I'll shoot, God help me I will."

The flashlight, juggled in his fingers tips and it fell into the snow as he tried to position the rifle correctly. He took aim at Tooth, but the beast didn't move a muscle. Edward tripped over a concealed root in the snow and the rifle went off sending a round hurtling into the trees. He scrambled to get to his feet and to readjust the rifle for another shot, but Tooth was on him and swept away the gun from his shaking hands. Edward screamed and ran, as fast as he could he headed back to the shack. He made the mistake of looking over his shoulder and he could see that Tooth was striding after him, with a burning hunger in his eyes and a determined grin on his face.

Edward slipped and fell, sprawling onto the freshly ploughed road and then scrambled towards his shack. He gazed around and could no longer see this creature, slamming the door of the shack shut and driving the lock into place as he fell against its flimsy corrugated structure breathing heavily. Nora looked at him confused, a tilt of her head made her ears flop, she had never seen him like this before and she did not know how to gauge such a strange reaction.

"Somebody...something is out there! Goddamn it, I have to tell the Sheriff." He switched on the CB transceiver and it was luckily still tuned into the correct frequency. Edward had never used the thing and had left it just how Sheriff Windwood had set it. There was white noise that met his ears, a sound that Nora didn't care for and she took cover under the armchair once again.

"Blasted thing!" Edward groaned, his head on a swivel, looking back at the door and the window.

"Hello, come in! Mayday! Mayday!" He said, not really knowing what it meant, but he had heard people say this in the movies a hundred times.

"Somebody help me!" He shouted into the receiver and then released the button to hear nothing but static as a reply.

The door burst open and Nora yelped as Beau Tooth stepped in through the door, he swept the armchair out of the way with his axe.

"NO!" Cried Edward.

Nora had seen enough and darted for the door, dodging a swipe from Beau Tooth's axe and swiftly zipping through the beast's legs and out of the shack.

"NORA!" Edward called out and again frantically tried to call for help, there was the sound of clicking on the other end and a voice said 'hello' only to be silenced by a falling axe. The CB transceiver exploded in a display of sparks and smoke and Edward backed off into the corner of his shack crying loudly as the wide silhouette of Beau Tooth smothered him.

Nora stopped halfway down Maple Drive, instinctively she turned back as if to return to help her friend, but then there was a scream so harrowing that she dismissed her first instinct and headed at full speed in the opposite direction.

CHAPTER 10

Sheriff Russell woke up in his chair at his desk like he had so many times before over the past year, a reoccurring habit that was becoming all too familiar. His head pounded, but this morning something was different, he awoke to the calming aroma of freshly brewed coffee. His nostrils twitched as he peeled himself from his desk and tried to focus.

"Finally!" Came a voice, someone was sitting on the other side of his desk, surrounded by a cloud of hot steam that rose up from a coffee cup. He tried to focus but his eyeballs were smothered in a transparent mucus that obscured his vision and the sound of the voice he did not recognise.

"I thought you were never gonna wake up."
He blinked away another drunken night's sleep and Agnes sat sipping the coffee.

"Urgh!" He groaned and dropped his head back to the desk.

"Happy to see me?" Agnes scoffed.

"Why won't you just leave me alone." He grumbled, his face pressed up against a pillow of papers.

"When you help me find the truth, I'll leave. But until then I'm your shadow."

Sheriff Russell sat up and leaned back in his chair, rubbing at his temples and trying to smooth out his hair that stuck out in a frenzy as though he had been electrocuted.

"I've told you what happened."

"You've told me parts. Other parts I have pieced together on my own from conversations with Dawn at the diner and Mister Hardwood at the bar."

"There's nothing I can…"

"I took the liberty of asking Deputy Clegg to make you a coffee. Black and sweet? I believe that's how you like it."

She slid the cup towards him on the desk, he said nothing but scooped the cup up and took a hefty swig. The buzz was instantaneous and his eyeballs expanded making him appear wide awake.

"You were in a right state last night." Agnes announced as she sat enjoying her coffee.

"I don't remember." He shrugged.

"We thought that this is where you would want to be when you woke up. So I got Mister Hardwood to bring you back here."

"Wait!" He exclaimed, "You've been here all night?"

"Yep." She grinned at him, loving that she was in control of matters. Sheriff Russell did not appreciate it and shifted uneasily in his seat.

"I don't think there was any need for you to do that."

"I didn't do it out of courtesy, believe me! I wanted to keep an eye on you. You know things that you're not telling me and I wasn't about to let you out of my sight. So when you're ready to spill the beans and tell me everything you know..."

"I've told you what I know."

"Bullshit!"

"Listen missy, you keep disrespecting me and you can spend a night in the cells for all I care."

"Disrespect?" Agnes burst out in a fit of hysterics and then shook her head.

"What's so funny?"

"I have to respect you first before I can show you disrespect, surely. And from what I have seen I find you and your actions downright appalling! You are supposed to be the Sheriff of this town, to hold the peace and keep the innocent safe and look at you!"

Her jab hit home, in fact it didn't just send him reeling onto the ropes, but it full on knocked him for a loop.

The referee would have been up to an eight count before he recovered from such a hit.

He couldn't deny her words either, because he knew she spoke the truth and she was only saying what was written in the eyes of those that dwelled in Maple Falls. Words that others would not speak were laid out abruptly by this stranger and they were words that he needed to hear.

"You're right." He murmured.

"Sorry? I didn't quite catch that.

"I said, you are right."

"About what?" She grinned smugly.

"Everything." He sighed, "I've let myself go and with it my grip on reality and what this town needs."

"Amen." She announced and lifted her coffee towards him in a gesture of agreement.

He stood up and stretched out his back, night after night of being slumped in his chair or draped over the desk had really started to play havoc with his posture and his spine was screaming at him for a night back in his own bed.

"So are you going to tell me what happened?" She asked, watching him closely as he walked over to a filing cabinet, slid open a drawer and retrieved a large folder that was stuffed full of papers, colourful post-its protruded out from it and flapped as he shook it in front of her.

"Here. Be my guest." He said, slamming the file on the desk.

"What's this?"

"The missing people file."

"Are you serious?" She gasped.

He nodded.

"Take a look." He gestured with his hand for her to open it up which she did eagerly.

Before her were pages and pages of photographs and information on all those that had gone missing in Maple Falls over the past twenty years.

"This is unbelievable!" Agnes said, shaking her head as she sifted through the faces of strangers.

"Keith W. Windwood, Elroy Pascoe, Lorraine Martel, Caroline Szopinski," He said as she swept passed photographs of all the lost, he didn't even look, it was as if he had memorised them all, "Paul Fernandez, Kenny Johnson, Max Fellows, Mia Chung, Robert Guy, Sophie Hewitt…"

These were names that she recognised and she slowed down her turning of the pages, knowing that any moment know she would be hit with a very familiar face.

"Dusty Greaves, Jessica Head." He continued almost aggressively in his tone.

"Stop it." Agnes whispered.

"Chester Duckworth!" He said.

"STOP IT!" Agnes cried, with tears in her eyes as she turned the final page and was met by her brother's large, doughy face and beaming happy smile. Sheriff Russell sighed and leaned on the filing cabinet, gazing out of the window.

"You wanted to know. So there it is."

"You didn't have to be so blunt." She snapped, wiping at her eyes with the sleeve of her oversized hoodie.

"I thought that was how you liked it? That is how you have been with me." He snapped back and then regretted his reaction and sighed again. "Look, I'm sorry for reacting like that. But you talk as though I don't care and nothing can be further from the truth, believe me. It's caring too much which is my downfall and that is what has broken me."

"Maybe I was wrong to judge you." She sniffed.

"We are human." He shrugged, "Judging is what we do."

"I apologise. I never knew there could have been so many missing people in such a small town. But why?"

"I thought you had been given that piece of the puzzle?"

"What do you mean?"

"Beau Tooth."

"Who is he?"

"A former resident of these parts apparently, before my time I'm happy to say. If the words of some of the locals are to be trusted and I do, I believe them, they have no reason to lie about such a thing. If what they say is gospel then he is responsible."

"What happened to him?" She asked.

"He was a lumberjack, fell on hard times and was behind on his work. Hauled up with his wife and two kids one winter as he tried to pull back some work through the off season. Well, they got snowed in and he went stir crazy as the story goes. He killed his family with an axe and then just up and disappeared."

Agnes had no words, but she covered her gaping maw with the palm of her hand.

"I told you your brother was dead and I believe that."

Agnes dropped her head, "I suppose it's too much to hope that he could be still alive out there after all this time."

Sheriff Russell sat back down and sighed.

"I believe every single missing person in that file has been murdered by Beau Tooth." He said, "And there's not a shred of evidence to corroborate any of it. Apart from the blood found at several scenes, we are yet to find any remains of the said victims."

"How does he do it?"

Sheriff Russell started to laugh, almost crazed and hysterical was the sound. He leaned back in his chair and swept his fingers through his hair and shook his head.

"That's what I'm trying to find out. And you know what? I'm stumped!"

"Maybe I could help you?" Agnes said with a wry smile, it was mischievous, but her eyes burned with determination.

"I don't know, we don't usually allow the general public to be involved in cases."

"Well, maybe you should." Agnes said, folding her arms and frowning at him, "I mean you haven't gotten very far on your own, have you?"

"Ouch." He laughed, "But true I suppose."

"I have degrees in human psychology and environmental geography and study cartography. I'm sure I could be of some help."

"Cartography?"

"Study of maps." She blushed, "Very nerdy I know."

"That may actually be of some use to me." Sheriff Russell pondered.

"So, can I be involved?"

He gazed at her for a moment, into those pleading eyes hidden by those thick spectacles of hers, behind her tough exterior he could see that there was just a scared kid who missed her brother.

"I just want the truth of what happened to my brother for my family's sake. Just give us closure, that's all I ask."

"Okay, you can help. As long as you realise I am in charge, not you!"

"Yeah, sure." She smiled.

"Well, before we start, I'm going to need some more coffee inside me." Sheriff Russell said, rising and heading for the door, "In fact, breakfast wouldn't go a miss. We can discuss the case at Dawn's. How about it? My treat."

Agnes's stomach rumbled.

"That sounds like a unanimous yes." Chuckled the Sheriff as Agnes apologised, her cheeks glowing brightly.

As the Sheriff opened the door to his office Deputy Clegg was there and it startled him.

"Jesus, Raymond! What have I told you about creeping about like that?"

"Sorry Sheriff." Deputy Clegg grinned, he held in his hands a piece of scrap paper with some writing scribbled on it.

"Anything come in during the night?" Sheriff Russell asked as he slipped on his coat and Agnes joined him with her oversized parka on. Deputy Clegg looked at her wide eyed as if something had been going on between the pair in the office.

"Raymond!" Russell snapped and the tone brought his gaze back to meet him.

"There was a call from Mrs Slapawitz, saying her Abe has gone missing."

"Missing?" Agnes exclaimed, fearing the worst.

"He took off ice fishing two days ago with Howie Kendal and hasn't been heard from since."

"Shit!" Growled the Sheriff, "I'll pay her a visit as soon as I can."

"Nate already did."

"Good. That saves me a trip. Has he filed a report?"

"Not yet, he is out on his morning rounds."

"Okay." Russell and Agnes walked down the corridor but Clegg cantered after them as if he still had more to tell the Sheriff, "We will be at Dawn's for breakfast. Miss Duckworth is going to be helping us with her brother's case."

"There's something else, Sheriff."

"What's that?"

"We received a mayday call on the transceiver last night."

"Mayday?" Sheriff scoffed, shaking his head as if anybody actually used such a call these days.

"It was very strange, I couldn't make any sense of it and it just cut off and I couldn't reach it on any frequency."

"Very odd."

"I can keep trying, see if anything comes up?" Clegg said as he stopped at the desk in reception. Sheriff Russell and Agnes walked out of the main doors into a gentle dusting of snow.

"You do that Raymond. Let me know if anything comes up."

CHAPTER II

Marlena Pascoe had suffered immensely since the disappearance of her husband Elroy, her mind had begun to wander and she had started to become very confused. Some days she believed that Elroy was still around and when she had days like these she went wandering herself trying to find him.

Sheriff Russell and Agnes Duckworth were about to get into the Sheriff's 4x4 when he noticed Marlena shuffling barefoot through the snow in nothing but a flimsy nightgown.

"Oh shit, not again." He sighed, slamming the door shut.

"What is it?" Agnes asked, stepping around from the passenger's side and then seeing this peculiar sight meet her eyes, "Oh!" She gasped, her brow furrowing with pity for the woman, who was visibly shaken and didn't seem to know where she was.

"Wait here, while I go and tend to her."

"Does this happen a lot?"

"Unfortunately, yes." He sighed and ran over to be at her side.

Marlena looked like some pale spectre, drained of life and purpose as she moved slowly through the snow up towards the high street of the town. Curtains twitched and eyes pitied her from the other side of the windows, hoping and praying that they never found themselves in the same situation as poor Marlena Pascoe.

Agnes wrapped her arms around herself and shuddered against the cold morning air, but she smiled at the tenderness of the Sheriff's touch as he draped his own parka around the poor woman's bare shoulders. Agnes realised there was indeed another side to Sheriff Russell, another layer to the drunken, broken one that she had met.

"C'mon now Marlena, what are you doing out in this weather?" Sheriff Russell asked her with hands rubbing at her arms that looked the colour and touch of porcelain. Vigorously he brushed at her arms trying to warm her up and get the circulation moving through them again.

"Elroy? Is that you, Elroy?" She asked, turning to face him, but her eyes were glazed and were gazing straight through him.

"No Marlena. It's me, Patrick. Patrick Russell."

"Patrick?" She said in a faraway voice, "Don't think I know anyone called Patrick. But I may be wrong, my mind does wander on occasions."

Sheriff Russell knew this was the understatement of the year, but was not cruel enough to make light of such a horrendous thing as dementia.

She had the early onset of Alzheimers even before her husband's disappearance, but since then she had become worse, whether the illness had been sped up due to having no one to talk to but herself or the trauma of such a loss. Who could say for sure, but this disease had consumed the jolly woman that Marlena Pascoe used to be.

"It's me Marlena, you remember me, The Sheriff."

"Oh, Sheriff Windwood." She exclaimed with a smile on her gaunt face, "How lovely to see you again, it's been a while."

"It has indeed." Sheriff Russell replied, deciding that it was easier to play along.

"You've looked better." She said, staring at his unshaven face with those heavy bags that always accompanied a heavy night on the liquor.

"You're probably right." He laughed, "C'mon, let's get you home. This ain't no place for you to be."

"Okay Sheriff, okay now." She stood holding his parka around herself, staring off into the distance at the snow tipped trees of Maple Woods.

The Sheriff quickly ran over to the vehicle where Agnes stood shivering.

"Is she going to be okay?" She asked.

"Yeah, well, as okay as she'll ever be I guess."

"What's wrong with her?"

"Dementia."

"Oh." She sighed, "I had an uncle that had that, it's very sad."

"It is." He agreed, "Do you think you can get yourself over to Dawn's and I will join you in a few minutes? I have to make sure to get her home and warm."

"Of course, I know the way from here."

"Okay. See you soon."

Before he left he opened up the car door and the glove compartment and took out a map of Maple Falls. It had been folded up so much that the creases in it had started to split, it was an old map indeed and he handed it to Agnes.

"Here! You like maps." He said, "Study this until I get back."

With that he turned around and Agnes stuffed the map into her rucksack as Sheriff Russell steered Marlena back towards her house which was not too far away.

Agnes trudged up the high street towards *Dawn's* diner, the last thing she heard Marlena Pascoe say was 'Are we going to see Elroy?' And she thought to herself what a cruel illness it was, in some ways it was worse for the sufferer's family and loved ones. They had to watch as their loved one's mind slipped away, the sufferer was oblivious to what was going on around them.

On the way back out of Marlena Pascoe's house Sergeant Nathan Brown pulled up at the side of the road and gave a quick short signal with his siren and lights, the strange high pitched whooping sound startled Sheriff Russell as he slipped back on his parka.

"Morning, Sheriff." Sergeant Brown said, winding down the window, "Paying house visits now are we?"

"Mornin' Nate. Yeah, something like that." He smiled.

"You'll get yourself a reputation you know, sneaking out of widow's houses in the early hours." Nate winked and laughed.

"I've already got a reputation, Nate." He laughed.

"Mrs Pascoe out on her travels again?"
Sheriff Russell nodded.

"Poor old girl." Nate shook his head.

"Where are you going?" Russell asked.

"Did Raymond tell you about some strange call that came over the radio last night?"

"He mentioned it, yeah. You know something I don't?"

"Well, I got to thinking that it could have only come from someone who has a CB transceiver, that was tuned to the office's frequency."

"Yeah." Russell shrugged.

"Well, if it wasn't one of us, which it wasn't. Then who was it?"

"Well, I'm damned if I know Nate. Someone with a CB transceiver."

"Exactly!" Nate exclaimed, "Before old Windwood went missing he gave out some CB radios to three men to help him keep tabs on what was going on around town."

"Who?"

"Elroy Pascoe," Nate nodded to the house behind him, "Chuck Muchnick and Eddie Gotch."

"Two of which are no longer with us." Sheriff Russell pondered.

"That's what I thought. So I'm just going to pay Eddie a visit and see if I can uncover anything. I mean it might not mean shit, you know how Raymond is, probably got it all wrong anyways. But I just thought I would check."

"Good thinking, get onto it."

"Where are you going anyway?"

"To Dawn's, I have a prior engagement."

"She's too young for you, Sheriff." Nate laughed.

"It's nothing like that!" He snapped, his cheeks glowing with embarrassment.

"Sure, sure." Nate smiled, "You want a lift?"

"No thanks, I think I'll walk." Sheriff Russell, zipped up his coat and positioned his ushanka hat into place as Nate drove away slowly up the high street, the chains wrapped around the tyres of the 4x4 crushing through the crust of untouched snow.

The snow fell down on Sheriff Russell's face as he started to trudge towards his destination.

"Yeah, I'll walk." He said to himself, "Hopefully it'll sober me up a bit."

CHAPTER 12

The snow around Maple Cross had already started to become thick and it would be due another visit from Mack Ferris and his snow plough. But that would be hours away, his route didn't bring him through Maple Falls until well past sundown. Sergeant Nathan Brown's 4x4 struggled to keep on the snow clad road, even with the chains wrapped around the tyres, he still had problems keeping the vehicle on the straight. The chains shredded through the top layer of crisp and pristine snow, the thick flakes fell and smothered his windshield as quick as the wipers could deflect them.

"Can't see shit out there." Groaned Sergeant Brown, "I'm going to have to go out on foot."
He pulled in on the corner of Maple Cross, sliding to a halt on the outskirts of the woods. The splaying branches of the redwoods above shielded the 4x4 from the worst of the falling snow and he stepped out into the bitterness.

He gazed around and shuddered, zipping his parka up to his chin and slipping on his ushanka hat. He was not a fan of this particular style of headwear, choosing to wear a campaign cover throughout the year, but in winter the ushanka was a necessity. If one was to stay out here too long then that chill bit hard and straight to your head.

He trudged through the ankle deep snow along the outskirts of the woods, staying close to the woods meant less snow.

"Fucking snow." He grumbled under his breath, "Can't stand the stuff."

He almost lost his footing on several occasions until finally he spied Gotch's shack in the distance.

"Finally." He shivered and moved onto the road, the snow was deeper but it had a crisp layer on top and it made it easier to walk through, there were too many protruding roots hidden on the path he'd been following, hence all the trips and stumbles.

"Remember that time you took a vacation to Florida?" He chuckled to himself, desperately trying to think of warming thoughts.

"Do you remember how hot it was? Sweltering, it was, so humid..." He sighed knowing that no amount of conjuring visions of old vacations was going to warm him at this moment in time, "...who are you trying to kid, Nate?"

He shivered and wrapped his arms around himself, hoping it would add a little extra warmth but it didn't.

"At least I can have a hot cup of Joe at Eddie's. His hospitality is always top notch. Good guy is Eddie Gotch. May even have something on the stove if I'm lucky."

Sergeant Brown licked at his lips with anticipation as he neared the shack. It was bent and crooked and slanted through the falling snow at a strange angle. The corrugated roof seemed to have so much snow on it that at any moment it would slide off in a miniature avalanche.

"Yeah and no doubt fall on my head." Scoffed Nathan Brown.

There was no sound on Maple Cross, but something stopped him in his tracks and he squinted to see through the curtain of thick falling snow. He could just make out the structure of the shack and realised that something was amiss.

"That's odd?" He said, noticing that the chimney wasn't coughing out its usual thick plumes of smoke from Eddie Gotch's stove that always seemed to be chugging away no matter the weather.

"He can't have gone out. Not in this." Sergeant Brown decided and quickened his pace as fast as he could to shuffle through the deepness of the snow.

"Mr Gotch! Eddie!" He called as he drew nearer. What was even more disturbing was that Nora hadn't started hollering to let old Eddie know that someone was approaching. Sometimes he'd fall asleep in his armchair and wouldn't hear visitors until Nora let him now.

"Eddie, you at home?" He called, all that met his ears was his own words reverberating around the trees. He suddenly had a very bad feeling, putting two and two together and coming up with more conundrums than answers. The mayday call from the evening before, now the deserted shack, Sergeant Brown was adamant that something had gone awry.

"Nora!" He called, trying a new tactic as he walked closer still, hand now gripping the handle of his sidearm, "C'mon girl, it's Uncle Nate, C'mon now Nora."

He whistled loudly, the sound attacked the snow clad leaves on the trees above him, but all the sound did was disturb a murder of crows that had been perched in the shadows surveying the Sergeant's peculiar behaviour. He watched them leave, their swiftness and high-pitched screeching saw him draw his revolver and he held it towards where they had sat in a nearby tree, only the falling of disturbed snow to aim at.

"EDDIE!" He called louder still as he arrived at the shack, he wanted nothing more than Eddie Gotch to be sitting in his armchair with Nora curled up at his feet, but somewhere in the pit of his stomach he knew, he knew that he would never witness that sight ever again.

The door was ajar, bent and twisted, almost grasping onto its hinges for dear life.

"Shit." He whispered to himself as he held the revolver out in front of him and he pushed the door slowly open. The door shrieked as if startled by the motion, then its misshapenness caused it to snag on the crooked floorboards. He was forced to open it the rest of the way with a well placed shoulder, causing it to scrape hideously across the uneven floor.

There was nothing and no one to greet him.

The stove was cold and unused, the television turned off but it was twisted on its stand into an unfamiliar position, Sergeant Brown could see from the dust buildup around the table where it normally sat.

"Strange." He murmured stepping into the shack.

There was nowhere for anyone to hide in such a small place, with only a curtain to separate the bedroom, which was in fact a cast iron bed with a dozen blankets on it. Sergeant Brown slid back the curtain, knowing that he wasn't there, but he had to look.

"Where the hell are you, Eddie?"

As he scanned the shack, he realised that more furniture had been disturbed and then spied the Citizen Band transceiver, or what was left of it. It had been caved in right through its centre, various coloured wires snaked out from its inside and jagged shards of circuit board protruded from its brokenness. The receiver hung from it on a coiled cable where it swayed gently from side to side in the bitter breeze.

"Something definitely went wrong here last night." Sergeant Brown said to himself before edging back towards the door.

He tore his radio receiver away from the velcro patch that held it to his chest and activated it, pressing a cold thumb onto the trigger. He was about to speak into it and inform the office that something had most definitely gone awry. But his eyes caught something in the snow that stopped him and he slowly placed his receiver back where it had come from, gripping his revolver tightly in his cold hands he stared at footprints in the snow that led to the rear of the shack.

The footprints were large and heavy, made with anger and determination, wide, too wide for the tread of Eddie Gotch he thought.

Sergeant Brown crept around the shack as he followed these tracks that looked fresh, he was adamant that he had not seen these tracks when he arrived. He tried to rack his brains.

Were those tracks here when I got here? I don't know for certain.

He continued to follow them until the falling snow was less flurry and more of a gentle sprinkle, where the snow became shallow and the road made way to the woods. He realised that he had moved deeper into the woods now and was approaching a clearing that was dusted with a fine layer of snow. Stood in its centre was an old rickety sledge. The wooden structure was stained with all manner of dark residue, as though paint had settled upon it and been allowed to dry untouched over a long period of time.

"Bit early for a visit from old Santa Claus." He scoffed, trying to delude himself about the situation, but his congested croaking voice betrayed him.

He gazed down at the trail made from the sledge's runners. Two straight lines slicing through the snow, leaving behind it a flaking trail of rust to corrupt the pristine pureness of the snow.

Sergeant Brown stopped in his tracks and surveyed the area, so deathly quiet was it that when the wind blew it sounded like the groan of some spectre sent to haunt him. The sound of such a sudden unexpected horror startled him and covered his neck with the sprouting of a thousand goosebumps.

It was then that Sergeant Brown noticed the cargo that the sledge was hauling. Curiosity getting the best of him, he stepped forward to remove the layer of snow that covered the contents and gasped as he unveiled such horrors. He staggered backwards, his eyes grew wide in disbelief, the dead, half frozen carcasses of three men lay piled on top of each other.

"Jesus Christ..." He whispered, as he saw the faces gaze back at him, the ghoulish charred face of Howie Kendal, his maw gaping and eyes wide as his final moments were captured for all to see.

Abe Slapawitz's head was split in two, like parting segments of a freshly peeled orange, but the cold had taken him and his flesh and blood was frozen a ghostly shade of blue.

"I...Oh, good God, I..." Brown gagged, trying not to lose his breakfast as he grabbed at his mouth to prevent any vomit from escaping his lips, he could feel it scratching at his throat, taste it on the back of his tongue.

There was so much to take in, every time he tried to close his eyes at the scene he found he couldn't and blinked rapidly, each time unveiling another horrific image that seemed to fuse itself into his mind's eye. Eyes open or closed he could never escape what lay before him.

Then he saw Edward Gotch.

"E-Eddie, Oh, Eddie, no..." Was all the words he had left, words formed by vomit and saliva that dribbled from his quivering lips.

The head of Edward Gotch hung to one side of his torso, almost completely hacked off, if it wasn't for the last few strands of tendon that hung on stubbornly then the head would have been rolling around the back of the sledge. Even more disturbing was the empty eye sockets that bled tears of blood, caught and frozen in time glistening like rubies.

"I've got to call this in, I've got..." Brown stuttered, so taken aback by the ordeal that he had forgotten what he had to do for a moment. He scrambled for his radio receiver blindly, not able to pull his gaze away from those barren eyes of Eddie Gotch.

This was a man that he would share a mug of coffee with when he was passing through, they would joke together and in the summer nights would sit outside with a lemonade and play a game of chess while the sun came down over the horizon. In many ways Eddie Gotch was Nathan Brown's best friend, knowing him from the days that they were both on the town's fire service. Something that Nathan Brown was still a part of, in a small town like Maple Falls you had to learn to split up your time and multitask, giving back to the community with whatever strengths you had was a must. Eddie had taken Nathan under his wing when he first joined up, but had been retired a fair few years now.

Now he was gone. Almost headless with his eyes gouged out and left to face eternity in complete darkness.

Sergeant Brown found himself thinking how terrifying it would be to dwell in purgatory without one's eyes, or would it be a blessing to not see the horrors that await?

There was a crunch of snow from the other side of the sledge and it startled Sergeant Brown back into action, immediately pointing his revolver in the direction of the noise, but he saw nothing. There was a grinding of chains, as rusted metal scraped against itself and then a sound of the thick linkage falling into the snow was muffled by the softness beneath.

"Who's there?" Sergeant Brown croaked, revolver shaking in his hands, "This is Sergeant Nathan Brown of the Maple Falls Sheriff's office. I strongly advise you to show yourself."

There was another sound of heavy footfalls in the snow and then nothing.

"Come out!" Brown barked, "With your hands behind your head!"

There was nothing, no sound or movement from the other side of the sledge.

A murder of crows suddenly appeared on a nearby branch that reached out above him, instinctively he looked up at the sound of their arrival. Their black eyes sparkled at him with knowing, a knowing of what was about to happen to him. They cawed at him almost mocking with their tone, laughter that left their beaks and circled around him that he could hear nothing else. His eyes flitted around the clearing and then back at the sledge, and the crows, his head spiralling as the sound of their laughter was all he could hear until it suddenly stopped and the massive bulk of Beau Tooth was standing in front of him.

Sergeant Brown froze and he slowly lowered his revolver, in horrified awe he gazed up at this mammoth of a man that towered above him. Beau Tooth was chewing on something, crunching something tough between his misshapen tusks that protruded from his rotting gums. Tooth smiled at him and the juices of whatever he was gnawing on dribbled from his chapped lips into his mass of dishevelled beard.

"I...I..." Was the only word that Sergeant Brown could muster, completely hypnotised by what he saw before him.

Beau Tooth's frostbitten digits, some of them missing finger nails, came into the Sergeant's eye line and between thumb and forefinger sat the moist eyeball of Eddie Gotch. Mucus and blood dripped from the sclera, that was now more pink than white from all the broken veins that had once snaked through it. The trail of mucus found its way down the dangling optic nerve that quivered in the cold breeze and hit the snow, spotting it with red droplets.

Sergeant Brown's eyes doubled when he realised what Tooth was holding and then continued to watch on in silent horror as this behemoth slid the eyeball in his cragged maw and bit down on it. The pop and then crunch was sickening and Sergeant Brown found himself going light headed as he staggered from side to side and fell against the sledge, his hand resting on the head of his friend Eddie Gotch. He gave out a scream and collapsed into the snow dropping his revolver. He gazed up at Beau Tooth as he closed in on him, his fingers curling into claws and creaking like his flesh was made of tough leather. The optical nerve hung from between Beau Tooth's lips and he smiled sadistically at the fallen Sergeant, before sucking the bloodied nerve through his lips as if it were nothing more than a strand of spaghetti.

"Oh, God, Oh..." Sergeant Brown whimpered as he felt vomit gurgling in the back of his throat, but he did not have long enough to unleash it as the meaty grip of Beau Tooth was quickly around his throat, forcing the bile to retreat from back where it had come from.

Sergeant Brown gasped for air, choking and gargling as saliva erupted from his mouth, his hands searching blindly in the snow for his revolver. The search was over when he finally seized it just as Beau Tooth hoisted him in the air by one hand and left him to dangle as Brown unleashed each round of his revolver. Six shots were fired, none hit home, the nearest cut through the fabric of Beau Tooth's checkered sleeve, sliding through the flesh of his arm beneath, but there was strangely no blood and it did not even seem to phase the deranged lumberjack. The majority of the bullets dug down into the snow below where his feet swung wildly in the air. Beau Tooth squeezed and his black fingers pierced the soft flesh around his throat and tugged at the tendons that were strung tight like the strings on a violin, one that would never make music again. Blood trickled down from the wound and splattered the carpet of white beneath as snow fell around the pair in the clearing, already the snowflakes were there to cover the monster's tracks as he claimed another victim.

Sergeant Brown choked but defiantly hung on to life and in a final act of pure desperation he managed to hold the gun up and aim it into Beau Tooth's face. It took all the effort he had left to hold the gun out, his shoulder burning with agony as he pulled the trigger again and again and again but nothing happened, nothing but the clicking sound of empty barrels as Beau Tooth erupted with a horrific sound of laughter.

Sergeant Brown gave up and his arm fell limp, dropping the gun into the snow once again, tears fell from his bloodshot eyes and blood seeped between Tooth's fingers.

His throat finally caved and his larynx hissed as warm air escaped into the cold and Brown's head wilted like a flower caught in the rain.

Beau Tooth tossed the carcass of Sergeant Brown on the back of the sledge and licked the fresh crimson from his fingertips, warm and thick and pleasing.

With the heavy chain in his hands, he draped it over his shoulder and began to heave it through the clearing, the runners gliding through the snow, leaving its rusty trail again. The crows above cackled angrily, unhappy that there were no leftovers for them, but they took to the air and followed Beau Tooth and his sledge as he moved slowly through the woods.

Sergeant Nathan Brown was on the verge of slipping away, but he was not dead just yet. Air escaped from his open throat like a gas pipe with an aggressive leak as he gazed at the dead faces that surrounded him.

He couldn't help his last thought being about Sheriff Russell and how he was right all along, and he silently cursed himself for not believing him.

As he gazed up at the trees above and the snow that fell all around him, he watched as the crows slid silently through the grey sky. He made one defiant act that he hoped could help his superior in his search for this monster and he grabbed with his twitching fingers his silver badge that clung to his parka. A star that homed a maple leaf in its centre, now smothered and stained with blood, a thumbprint pressed in it on purpose before he tore it away from the material and dropped it into the snow as the sledge slowly continued on its journey as Sergeant Brown's journey came to an end. The badge remained in the snow, shimmering like a beacon, waiting and hoping for someone to find it.

CHAPTER 13

The coffee was hot and much needed as Sheriff Russell and Agnes sat in a booth at *Dawn's* around the large map of Maple Falls. Dawn had made sure to keep the pair topped up but had not interrupted in their endeavour to find something on that map that may help them discover the whereabouts of the elusive Beau Tooth.

"The green dots that I made were possible dwellings where I believed he could have been hiding." Sheriff Russell said pointing to the random spots of green marker pen.

"And the red crosses were places you have checked? I take it?" Agnes replied, fanning her hand out across the map over a mass of red crosses that seem to overwhelm it.

"Unfortunately, yes." Russell sighed, scratching at his head.

"You still maintain that he crosses the lake to get here?" Agnes asked, sipping her coffee and pondering the map.

"Yeah," He nodded, "absolutely. I can't think of any other way. The disappearances only ever happen during the Winter months and only when Old Syrup freezes over. So he must be coming over from Blackfoot Ridge or Black Leaf."

Sheriff Russell automatically pointed out the places on the map that were circled in blue marker pen, both of them on the other side of the lake.

"And you say that your relationship with Blackfoot's authorities have become strained?"

"Strained!" Russell nearly choked on his coffee as he laughed, "Strained is one word for it. I pestered the hell out of them until they did a statewide search."

"And did they?"

"Well, they said they did, but I wasn't sure and now well, I've been blackballed by their Sheriff as a troublemaker, so I have lost their support on the matter."

Agnes stood up and wandered around the table, to take in another angle of the map.

"Do you think it could be possible that he lives in Pepperville? Or Haast?"

"I hadn't thought about the possibility of him coming from neighbouring towns." Sheriff pondered for a moment.

"So, it is a possibility?"

"Personally I think it could be too far a journey for him to travel. But it's definitely something I could look into. Sheriff Shaw of Haast is usually quite accommodating and I have never had any dealings with Sheriff Beverly of Pepperville."

"Well at least that's something to go on."

"Yeah, it all depends if Sheriff Delaney of Blackfoot has reached their ears and warned them to stay away."

Sheriff Russell made a note of it on his notepad, while Agnes continued to examine the map.

"How did you come to the realisation that he came across the ice? I mean he may well live here in Maple Falls."

"No, that makes no sense or he would be out there all weather wreaking havoc surely."

"I guess that makes sense." Agnes agreed.

"It was one eyewitness that I believe had an encounter with Tooth a few years ago."

"And lived to tell the tale?" Agnes gasped.

"Well, it was a University professor, a Professor Cumberbatch. He wrote a piece on the urban legend known as the Blackfoot yeti that is said to dwell in these parts."

"Yetis!" Chuckled Agnes with a dismissive role of her eyes.

119

"Yeah, well, he ventured out into the wilderness and he found something else, but unfortunately refused to go into detail about it."

"Have you spoken to him?"

"Believe me, I've tried." Russell sighed, "No doubt another member of the 'I Blackballed Sheriff Russell' fan club." He laughed.

"Maybe that's another lead worth exploring?"

"I've tried calling him and emails…"

"Perhaps you've just gotta bite the bullet and pay him a visit."

"Like you, you mean?"

"Yeah and look where it got me." She winked and he smiled, before they both took a moment to sip their coffee, before Sheriff Russell added it to his notes of things to do.

The map was torn in places and the creases veined into the folds making some areas difficult to read.

"Do you have another map? This one has seen better days don't you think?" Agnes said, holding it up by a corner and watching it tear away in her hands.

"Be careful with that!" He moaned and snatched it out of her hands only to cause more damage to it.

"Well, don't you have another one? I picked up this one from the motel, but it hardly has any of the places on it that this older one does."

"Back at the office, sure, but..." He looked over at Dawn who was leant on the countertop talking to Wendy Hardwood who was sipping a honey and lemon tea.

"Dawn!" He called.

"Yes, Sheriff?"

"Do you have a map of Maple Falls?"

"I may have one somewhere..." Dawn pondered for a moment, trying to recall its whereabouts.

"Never mind." Agnes interrupted and started to unzip her rucksack, "I've got something better."

Dawn shrugged and went back to talking with Wendy and Sheriff Russell looked at her with intrigued eyes.

"What have you got there?" He asked.

"Ta da!" Agnes exclaimed, unveiling a laptop, "Welcome to the 21st century Sheriff."

"Oh very funny." He scoffed, "I'm not a dinosaur you know."

She paid no attention and flipped open the lid and immediately it burst into life. It took her a moment to adjust the wifi settings and then she was away. Her fingers skipping across the keys expertly with ridiculous speeds that blew the Sheriff's mind. He wasn't that old, but technology moved by so quickly these days that it had left him standing still trying to figure out cell phones. The youth of the day were brought up with such contraptions and could work them with ease leaving the generation before playing catch up.

"Here we go." Agnes said and spun the laptop around to face the Sheriff.

He gazed at the screen taking in Maple Falls in all its glory.

"Here let me show you." Agnes said sliding into the booth next to him and expertly using the built in mouse to zoom in on various places.

"Well, isn't that something?" He chuckled to himself.

"If you think that's something then watch this." She zoomed back out with a flick of her fingers and hovered around the high street before zooming straight into the town and moving the angles around so all the shop fronts were visible.

"Well I'll be damned!" He chuckled, "Can you do this for the woods?"

"Unfortunately not as close as this due to the street view cars unable to get through, it's usually only places that have roads that we can really get a good look at."

"That's a pity." He sighed, feeling like it was another one step forward three steps back scenario.

"But maybe if I went on Earth…" She said to herself and worked her magic again on the laptop until the planet Earth appeared, she zoomed rapidly in on

Maple Falls as if they were a comet hurtling words earth then she halted the camera at a pixelated view of the lake and woods.

"Whoops too far." She said and pulled the image back to where trees and water could be made out.

"The things that you kids have at your disposal nowadays."

"It's at your disposal too, Grandpa!" She chuckled.

"Hey!" He laughed.

"Well that's as clear and as close as I can get it."

"Can you just scan the areas that I have marked in green and see if anything looks suspicious?"

"I sure can."

The screen showed the various places that Sheriff Russell had marked as possible places for Beau Tooth's whereabouts, but it showed nothing of any importance. They sat in silence as they went over each site, Dawn approached and filled up their mugs but they didn't even notice.

Sheriff Russell leaned back in his seat and sipped his coffee, sighing as the last spot showed them nothing of any interest.

"I was positive that surely one of those places would have been it."

"Sorry, Sheriff." Agnes sighed.

"Never mind, back to the drawing board I guess..." But just had the words left his lips and coffee caressed them, it was spat out, spraying the air and causing Agnes to flinch away from him in disgust.

"Jesus!" She wailed.

"Go back, go back there!" He said excitedly.

"Where?" She asked as she moved the cursor around over the lake.

"There! Look there! Over Fisherman's Island"

She halted the cursor and over Fisherman's Island there seemed to be some kind of discrepancy in its centre as though a cloud hung over it.

"Zoom in, zoom in!" He cried.

"Okay, okay, what is it?" She asked.

They zoomed in as close as they could without distorting the image and there stood a small squared structure, with plumes of smoke above it.

"Smoke." He whispered.

"Smoke, as in a fire?" Agnes asked.

"As in a chimney!" He exclaimed.

"But surely Fisherman's Island has been checked thoroughly before?"

"Well, yes, but..." He pondered and realised that he had never searched the island himself.

"What is it?"

"I haven't been there myself, but the files of Sheriff Windwood said it had been searched when he was onto something himself..."

He interrupted himself and snatched his radio receiver from its position on his jacket and spoke excitedly into it.

"Raymond, are you there? Come in Raymond."

There was a pause as if there would never be an answer.

"Goddamn it Deputy Clegg, where are you?"

"Sorry, Sheriff." Came the reply through a flurry of static, *"I was in the John."*

"Never mind that!" Russell snapped, "Listen I want you to pull up the files on the computer."

"Okay." Clegg responded, nonchalantly, sounding as though he was chewing on something.

"Are you eating on the job, Raymond?" Sheriff Russell growled.

"I gotta eat Sheriff!"

"Okay, okay. Are you logged in?"

"Yes, Sir."

"Search for Sheriff Windwood."

"Okay. Done. What am I looking for exactly?"

"What was the last report he filed?"

"Erm, one of the missing people ones."

"Did it have a location?"

"Fisherman's Island."

Agnes and Sheriff Russell looked at each other with wide eyes.

"It was, oh that's weird..." Clegg said through the sound of loud mastication.

"What?"

"This was the day before he disappeared."

"Thank you Raymond, Sheriff out!"

They turned to each other in excitement.

"So Sheriff Windwood found something on Fisherman's Island, went back the next day and was never seen again." Agnes said.

"My God, he's on Fisherman's Island. The bastard's been there all this fucking time!" Russell growled and slammed a fist down on the table, spilling his coffee in the process.

"There's no time to be feeling guilty now, Sheriff." Agnes said standing up and putting on her parka.

"Where do you think you are going?" He asked as he stood up quickly and did the same.

"Fisherman's Island. I'm going to find this fuck and put a bullet in his head!" She said unveiling a strange, bulbous looking gun from her rucksack.

"Oh, no you're not!" He said, snatching the gun out of her hand. "And where the hell did you get this from?"

"My dad's garage at the lake house."

"Jesus, Agnes, this is a flare gun! You shoot him with this and he'll have no fucking head left!"

"Good!" She snapped, snatching the flare gun back from him, "That's exactly what he deserves."

"You can't go." Sheriff Russell, said calmly, "I can't allow it."

"But..." Agnes was ready to argue her corner, when he placed a hand on her shoulder.

"I failed your brother, Agnes." He said, "I don't want to fail you too."

Her eyes became glazed and her large spectacles seemed to magnify the tears and give the illusion that her eyes were submerged in a tank of water.

"Please stay here." He pleaded.

She nodded as she snivelled and Dawn arrived at her side and put an arm around her.

"She'll be safe here, Sheriff." Dawn said, "I'll look after her."

"I have a chance to make this right!" Sheriff Russell said as he rushed from the diner.

"That's all we want to do." Dawn said to herself as the Sheriff fled the diner.

"What did you say?" Agnes asked, lifting her teary eyes up and wiping away mucus from her nostrils.

"I have a lot to tell you." Dawn sighed and in her own eyes there was the swelling of tears.

CHAPTER 14

Sheriff Russell hurtled along hidden roads that were now nothing more than snow and ice, getting colder and more hazardous still as evening approached. He knew that he should slow down, that the speed he was travelling in the 4x4 was outlandish, but his mind was racing and he believed that he had already lost too much time. People may have already fallen to Beau Tooth's axe and with each fatality it became another thread of guilt that wrapped itself around his gut in an unyielding knot.

The chains that had been wrapped around the vehicle's tyres helped to grip the layer of snow and somehow kept the Sheriff on the road, but there were some moments where he knew he was riding his luck. He was thankful when he arrived at the opening to the woods at the old dirt road that led to the Lumberjack's Cabins, there was no way he would be able to get up that road in his 4x4 and he cursed himself for not having a Bobcat snowmobile fuelled and ready to go, it would have definitely made the journey a swifter one. Instead he slid out of the vehicle and scooped up the shotgun that had been nestled between the two front seats and he headed up the path into the woods.

The snow was thick and shin deep, but not as bad as it would get after a week's worth of this weather. Trudging up the usual dirt road that was now a thick sheet of untouched white, he was stabbed with the sharp blade of déjà vu.

"Last year." He wheezed as he moved as fast as he could through the snow, "Last year in the same blasted place."

It was a memory that he could never forget, there was more snow then and the journey took a lot longer and was far more physically taxing than now, but it was the outcome that caused that knot of guilt to twist and tighten and bring back the memories of last Winter's ordeal.

"I was too late." He hissed, words seeping out on a cloud of vapour from his taut lips, it was said with anger and his teeth ground together to create a horrid sound.

Last year he had been too late and seven teenagers lost their lives at the hands of Beau Tooth, or if you were to believe the official reports on the matter, seven 'disappearances' but Sheriff Russell no longer believed such reports.

He had found signs of scuffles, a large amount of blood at the scene which belonged to some of the victims and most horrifically a human scalp. DNA identified that the scalp belonged to a Miss Mia Chung, but without a body the powers that be still would not shake off the missing person tag. A vintage 1983 Vandura cargo van had been left destroyed too and with closer inspection it was clear that it had been besieged by a heavy and sharp instrument, forensics had said something with a steel head like a pick, sledgehammer or an axe. Still Sheriff Russell found that his hands were tied which caused him to slip even more into this dark period of his life. It was a desperate need to uncover the truth that drove him on for the last twelve months and what drove him on now through snow and ice and the aching of burning muscles as he approached the cabins.

There was no sign of life from the vacant cabins, roofs smothered in a thick layer of snow like some gingerbread house in a fairytale. Sheriff Russell passed them by without even a second thought or glance, for two reasons, there were too many bad memories attached to the inside of one cabin in particular and he had already spent too much of his time reflecting on what happened there. The second reason was that he had shut Dawn's letting of the cabins in the Winter months down, there would be no more poor lambs led to be slaughtered, not on his watch.

He soon found himself on the banks of Old Syrup where he stopped for a moment to catch his breath and find his composure, he had to have a clear head or things could go from bad to worse very quickly.

His boots crunched on the hardened mud as he looked out at the frozen lake, the small island known as Fisherman's stood a mass of trees and snow. The island was a cocoon with each season that came and went, Spring and Summer it was smothered with the radiant greens and yellows of all manner of leaves. When Fall arrived a mass of fallen leaves had acted as the shell to hide what lurked within and now the Winter, the snow was Beau Tooth's friend, it kept him safe and unfound on the island and covered his tracks just how he liked it.

Sheriff Russell breathed in to calm himself down, the adrenaline was bubbling up inside him and was threatening to sweep through his body at any moment, he couldn't allow it too, not yet.

He gripped the shotgun tightly in his hands, the metal barrel and wooden comb cold against his skin, but he welcomed it, his skin had become clad with a layer of nervous sweat.

With a staggered exhale he began walking across the frozen ice of the lake, a fine layer of snow had settled upon it and he kicked it away with each step he took. The sun had settled away behind the mountains of

Blackfoot now and bathed the cloudy sky in tones of pink and red.

"Red sky at night..." He said to himself as he made his way across the frozen lake.

He paused for a moment to take in the scene he had investigated just a few days ago, the broken remnants of the shanty that had been left strewn across the ice. Remembering his conversation with Sergeant Brown earlier with the news that Howie Kendal and Abe Slapawitz had not returned home from an ice fishing trip. He realised now that they were dead.

"Goddamn them!" He growled, continuing towards his destination, "If only people would have paid attention to my warnings."

Beau Tooth had struck again and taken the lives of two more citizens of Maple Falls, but there was nothing he could do about that now, the only thing he could do was stop him from taking anymore lives.

"Perhaps I should have been harder on them all? More severe punishments. They already hate me, I should have given them a true reason to."

His musing had sent his mind to a different place, a world where he had made all the right decisions and the town lived in perfect harmony, a fantasy world. So captivating was this vivid daydream that he did not realise that he had reached Fisherman's Island.

His boots crushed down on a layer of dead leaves left over from fall, covered in a crystallised layer of frost, the crunching sound was enough to wake him up.

His heart rate quickened and his brow was lacquered with sweat, but he stepped forward into the mass of trees and shrubs that seemed to wrap around him in a twisting labyrinth of branches.

CHAPTER 15

Sheriff Russell crept cautiously through the dried and twisted shrubbery, the weather conditions had not been kind to plant life, forcing whatever grew inside to retreat and cower within its hardened twisted branches. Yes, the plant life had become used to this annual onslaught and had evolved with its cruelty, knowing when to shy away and lay dormant. Sheriff Russell however didn't understand that, he had not lived in the town of Maple Falls long enough yet to truly understand the effect that Winter had on this place. After being caught and groped several times by the jagged reaching claws of branches and thorns he finally arrived at a clearing on the island. If he had had his wits about him at that moment in time he could have taken the constant barrage of attacks from the flora as a warning. Did the branches pull at his parka as a warning? Did the thorns prick his flesh out of care? Did the vines wrap around his feet and ankles to hold him close and halt his expedition? Warnings to stay clear, to turn back and return to the town of Maple Falls, strong warnings to possibly even leave the town altogether and return to the safety of the life he once knew in the quiet town of Crimson.

But he would do no such thing, for he did not heed the warnings, he was blinkered like a racehorse who only had one thing on its mind and that was finishing the race. The Sheriff's race finally came to an end when he stumbled out into the clearing and was met by a misshapen shack constructed from all manner of various woods and metal. One of the walls had been created from a large metal sheet, a sign that welcomed newcomers or those passing through to Maple Falls. Sheriff Russell had remembered how difficult it was to find Maple Falls when he had first arrived there and the reason was because this particular sign had been stolen. It had since been replaced, but he had thought nothing of it until now.

"Good God, he was here all along." His whisper suddenly turned into a growl and he was more angry at himself for not thoroughly investigating the area.

"Damn the bastard, he's been mocking me."

Sheriff Russell's cheeks flushed as vibrant as two ripe raspberries, but it was embarrassment that he felt at this moment in time, he could feel the heat creeping up the back of neck. He hated feeling like this, knowing that he could have done something about it sooner and instead couldn't see the wood for the trees, he couldn't see what was straight in front of him all this time.

"Should have opened your damn eyes, Patrick!" He growled and then the embarrassment seemed to wash over him as a cold wintry chill welcomed him back to reality and the here and the now.

He cocked the shotgun and approached the shack with caution. He made sure to survey the construction first, he didn't want to be ambushed or this interaction could be over before it even started. The holes cut in it acting as windows were either shuttered or covered with plastic or tarpaulin. Tarpaulin had also been used on the roof along with misshapen boards and corrugated steel. The roof was currently layered with snow, with the remnants of grass and moss underneath which would have made the roof appear green and blend in during the spring and summer months.

Sheriff Russell speculated that this is why the helicopters that had been sent out during the missing persons search had found nothing out of the ordinary when passing over the island.

He tried to peek in through the cracks of the shack's walls but saw nothing but gloom and stepped back to survey the structure once again. He noticed the makeshift chimney that rose from the misshapen roof and a part of him was relieved not to see plumes of smoke flowing out into the sky.

"He's not here." He said to himself and lowered his defences, pointing his shotgun down towards the ground, the barrel of the gun looked almost sad as it drooped down facing the snow, but as much as Sheriff Russell would have liked to burst in there and plow a slug right between the bastard's eyes, he didn't know how he would react when he finally met this monster face to face.

Would he freeze? Would he flee? He honestly couldn't say.

He found the door and pushed it open, the hinges sang a rusty chorus and he stepped into the gloom of the shack. It was difficult for him to make anything out in the gloom with just random shards of light creeping through holes of the shack. He stood in the darkness for a moment and took in the world of Beau Tooth. The smell of damp and earth mixed with urine and faeces was nothing compared to the stench of stale, rotting flesh and the hint of blood in the air that scratched at the back of his throat and nostrils. A shudder worked its way up and down his spine and he searched blindly for his flashlight that hung from his belt, his fingers quivered and struggled to find the switch, but when he finally did and a beam of light burst from it, it illuminated the roaring maw of a grizzly bear that caused him to cry out and stagger backwards, trip up and fall on his backside in the trodden earth. The flashlight fell too and sat pointing up at the face of this bear that was frozen in time. He breathed a sigh of relief when he realised that the creature wasn't alive and he picked himself up and dusted himself off again left to feel embarrassed. He lifted the flashlight up and aimed it at the bear, at closer inspection he could see that it was nothing more than the pelt and a head, hanging from a nail on the wall of the shack. As the flashlight drifted around the walls he saw more trophies of elk, cougar and wolverine mounted, their marbled eyes shimmering in the flashlight. He stepped back and his hip bumped against something hard and he realised it was a stove, he slid the flashlight around until he found a makeshift table which was in fact an upturned wooden crate.

"That's what I'm looking for." He said to himself as he found a liquid fuelled lantern and spent a few moments readying it before slipping a match from a matchbox that sat next to it and lighting the lamp. A few adjustments to the flame made the shack erupt with a warming amber glow and then he was able to see the true world of Beau Tooth.

A gasp left Sheriff Russell's gaping maw with such length and emphasis that there was a moment that he believed it may well have been a leak in the lamp. He turned around and was met by other trophies, the human remains rose up in neat piles, each specific bone was matched to its own kind. Tibias were piled with tibias, femurs with femurs, vertebrae (most of them

138

were fully intact) piled together and then the skulls, too many to count balanced on top of each other.

"Jesus..." was all he could find to say, what else could he say faced by such a morbid monstrosity. He turned away when he realised that some of those hollowed sockets belonged to people he had once known, that was too much to take in at this moment in time. As he turned around to explore the shack, the stove was present and was stacked with freshly cut logs next to it. In the far corner a makeshift bed had been constructed out of pallets and on top of it were layer upon layer of animal pelts, from all manner of animals. Something caught his eye in a corner of the shack, it was what appeared to be clothes all folded up neatly in a pile, wrapped in a plastic sheet. He approached it and took out his penknife and quickly sliced through the plastic, he ripped it apart and felt what he believed was clothes within, he was mistaken. He flinched from the sensation that met his touch, the coldness and texture shocked him for it was not what he had expected at all. He reached in and pulled out this strange textile and held it up to the light before realising it was a sheet of human flesh that had been peeled off one of his victims.

"Shit!" He gagged, vomit filling the back of his throat as he released what he held in his hands and let it fall back into the plastic bag with the other pieces.

139

Then on a mound of clothes, that he believed were those of the victims, was a full suit that had been threaded together by string, twine and fishing wire. The size of such a bodysuit was gargantuan when compared to his frame and size and as he stepped forward he realised it was made from the victims that had fallen to Beau Tooth's axe.

"T-That's how he survives the cold. An extra layer of skin." His face contorted as he grew nearer, examining it and all manner of shades and textures all knitted together to create this inhuman monstrosity. It was when he saw the tattoo of an eagle over a maple leaf that he knew belonged to Sheriff Windwood he staggered back.

"W-Windwood..." He remembered the Sheriff getting dressed in the locker room and him explaining what the tattoo had meant on his arm.

'We had all got them done after serving in Iraq for the Canadian army.' He recalled.

He spent the next several moments gagging and coughing, saliva hanging from his lips and hitting the earth below as he was doubled over in disbelief and sickened horror.

"What kind of a sick bastard are you?" He spluttered as he stood up and spat the last gob of spit into the soft earth below.

He felt light headed it was all too much for him, he had never expected this, he hadn't known what to expect if he was being completely honest. But it wasn't this, it could never have been this.

He leaned on a large cast-iron cooking pot that stood next to him cradled on top of a second stove, this one used for cooking. As he steadied himself his fingers slipped into the broth that had presumably been cooked not too long ago for it was still warm. He recoiled and looked inside the cauldron and saw a thick liquid that quivered with reds and browns, he wiped his fingers on his trousers to rid himself of whatever it was that they had just been smothered in. A ladle protruded out from it and curiosity got the best of him and he moved the broth with the utensil, disturbing it and bringing chunks of something that resembled meat to the surface. He lifted the ladle and saw pieces of meat and brain in it.

"Goddamn it!" He heaved and dropped the ladle back into the cauldron, frantically wiping his hand on his trousers. He had seen enough and scrambled around for a way out, he found a doorway that led out to the rear of the shack through several curtains of various materials.

He found himself outside again and frantically breathing in that fresh air that had a cold bite that was much needed to cleanse the aromas that had clung to the hair in his nostrils and were refusing to leave. Each smell was disgusting and tickled his brain with a new sickening memory of what lay behind those dishevelled walls.

"I never thought it would be like this." He gasped, with his hands on his thighs trying to breathe. He stood back up and looked up to the sky and allowed the snowflakes to fall upon his face and soothe him, calm him. He wished that with each kiss of a snowflake on his tacky flesh that it would take away a vision of what he had witnessed from within the shack, but he knew it was a waste of time.

"Wishing for things is for kids." He said and sighed, the only thing he really wished for was for his wife to come back, she always knew the right thing to say, he was nothing without her and realised that now.

"The first thing I do after all this shit is done is call her. I need to make it right with her."
The words had only just left his lips when he realised that this was still far from over and he gazed across the frozen lake back towards Maple Falls.

"But what will he do now? There's no one here for him, no lambs led to be slaughtered. Where will he..."
His eyes caught the marks in the snow of where a sledge had sat and he quickly followed the tracks down

to the bank and the lake where they appeared as chipped and scratched lines on the surface of the ice.

"Oh, God no!" He gasped and set off as fast as he could across the ice back towards town. Realisation had struck him like a wrecking ball between the eyes that without those lambs that were being gifted to the beast then there was only one place that Beau Tooth could go in search of his harvest.

"He's heading for town!"

CHAPTER 16

As darkness fell on Maple Falls the surrounding woods grew relatively quiet, the odd whistle of a Red-tailed Hawk circling for one last meal for its supper before retiring to its nest. The hoot of a Great Horned Owl heading out for an evening of untold adventures. Or even the shuffle of a gaze of racoons as they made their way through shrub and snow into town on the lookout for unattended garbage cans.

One peculiar sound that joined these nocturnal imps on their evening rituals was the sound of a chain scraping upon the rusty chassis of an old sledge, splintered boards of brown and dark, flecked with the droplets of crimson from several years of wrath.

The rusted runners slowly carved through the thick layer of untouched snow leaving behind two perfectly straight lines of flaked rust.

The sledge came grinding to a halt and the heavy breaths of such arduous labour were obvious and for a moment he could do nothing but recuperate. Inhaling the cold night air that was flecked with the falling of snowflakes and ice into his black lungs, snow melting immediately on just sensing the darkness within. He exhaled in a cloud of thick breath that resembled the black plumes of smoke that erupt from the chimney stacks of old steam trains. There was congestion within his throat at each breath, as though his throat was filled with tar that was impossible to clear no matter how much he growled.

He gazed at the lights that flickered before him, street lamps glowing brightly, illuminating a world he had not seen in many years. A street of white, dozens of lines sliced through it where some vehicles had driven, while other vehicles sat idly, sleeping outside various buildings. These buildings were alive with light too, behind each pane of glass the silhouettes of people who went about their business unbeknownst of the horrors that awaited them. Bright neon signs flickered looking to lure the weak-minded inside with their flamboyant temptations.

Beau Tooth's mismatched eyes squinted, the bright lights seemingly too much for his delicate eyes, eyes that had spent the past twenty years in the gloom of nothingness or the coldness of snow, such things were alien to him now, a world he left behind a long time ago.

He lifted the heavy chain and heaved the sledge out from the confines of the woods and into the high street.

145

The street sat in silence as he moved slowly onto the road, slicing through the tracks made by car tyres with its rusted trail. He finally stopped and let the chain fall and become buried in the snow beneath, before trudging round to the rear of the sledge. For a moment he took in his harvest, he seemed to ponder for the longest time, staring at the twisted remains of corpses that were piled within, freezing blood turning to icicles. Could it be that the behemoth was taking this moment to think about all the horrors he had committed? Could his conscience be pricking at him to tell him that this harvest was enough and would see him through to next winter, was this enough for all his needs and wants?

Beau Tooth instead smiled, a disgusting smile, saliva forming on his crooked teeth and dribbling down into his beard that was caked with dried blood, meat and other unexplained crusted stains.

If he did have a conscience then it was out of order, like an old phone box that had been demolished by vandalism and left useless and unrepairable. He gazed back at the surrounding buildings as he stood under the street lamps as if the spotlight had been shone on him and created his own form of art for all to see.

The smile disappeared and there was hatred and anger that creased his scarred face. He balled his fists tightly, fingers creaking and cracking, he had felt confused at first as to why there was no offering for him this winter, no easy pickings like there had been for the past seventeen years. It had taken a few years for the citizens of Maple Falls to catch on and for the past few years had turned a blind eye to people visiting the woods during the cold season, in some cases even forceful in their persuasions for outsiders to visit the wonders of the Maple Woods in the winter. In some ways those that had done such a thing were worse than anything Beau Tooth could do with an axe, but that is something that they must live with for the rest of their days, days that may well be numbered.

Laugher erupted down the sidewalk as a bunch of rowdy men trudged along, slapping each other on the backs and pushing and shoving immaturely before disappearing inside *Chopper's Bar*. None of the men noticed Tooth or his sledge, most of today's society so wrapped up in their own lives and their own bullshit to even notice a deranged man with murder on his mind and sledge filled with broken corpses.

He grinned and looked around again, his eyes twinkling like a child in a sweet shop, the harvest awaited him, it was all here for the taking and take it he shall.

He slid the bloodstained axe from the sledge and twirled it around in his meaty hands before gazing at the chunks of frozen flesh and blood that clung to it as though it was fusing with the steel and becoming part of the axe itself.

147

He swirled it through the air as if it were a practice swing and let it cut through the delicate snowflakes that fell in a gently flurry. The axe settled on his shoulder as he cradled it there and turned to his left, boots disturbing the snow at his feet and he gazed at the diner that was ablaze with light, silhouetted behind the glass danced for him in a frenzy of movement. Beau Tooth smiled again and moved towards the diner with eagerness.

CHAPTER 17

The slap sounded like a gunshot and the impact caused an already weeping Dawn Rougeau to stagger back on her heels and collapse into one of the booths. Agnes stood holding her wrist, her fleshy palm stinging from the impact as the sound of the blow still echoed around the empty diner. Dawn sat up with tears streaming down both her cheeks, one of them a throbbing red blemish as she cradled it in her shaking hand.

"How could you?" Agnes growled, shaking with adrenaline and exasperation, she gazed at her hand, her palm was throbbing almost as identical as Dawn's cheek.

Dawn said nothing in return, but buried her face in her hands and sobbed loudly.

"Stop it!" Agnes spat, tears streaming down her own cheeks now as if mocking Dawn's own grief.

"I'm sorry, I..." Dawn snorted and spluttered, shaking her head that was still cradled in her hands.

"Stop this!" Agnes hissed, lifting her spectacles and wiping away the tears from her own eyes with the back of her hand. She strode across the diner and seized her parka and quickly slipped it on, before stuffing her laptop and map into her rucksack.

"Where are you going?" Dawn sniffed, looking up from her hands.

"What the hell is it to you?" Snapped Agnes.

"But, Sheriff Russell told you to stay here."

"With you?" She scoffed, "Fat chance! I think I would sooner take my chances with Beau Tooth than stay in the presence of a lying, poisonous snake like you!"

Agnes zipped her rucksack in such anger that the teeth of it caught on the fabric and she struggled frantically to undo it.

"But, you can't go, it's too dangerous." Dawn pleaded, standing up and sliding out from behind the booth's table.

"Stay the hell away from me!" Agnes growled.

"Let me help you..." Dawn said, approaching her with reaching hands and eager fingers to help her with her bag.

"Leave me alone!"

"I..." Dawn approached closer still, Agnes did not move, perhaps she didn't really want to move, perhaps she didn't want to be mad at Dawn at all.

"I mean it!" Agnes threatened, but made no attempt to move away from the oncoming Dawn.

"Let me help, you're struggling." Dawn sighed, her tone was gentle and caring.

"I said..." Agnes growled, but there was no fight left in her tone, no matter how hard she tried.

Dawn took the rucksack from her and slid it across the table of the booth and began to tamper with the zip.

"I..." Agnes sighed and collapsed onto a chair and dropped her head, "I just can't believe you could have done such a thing. That was my brother and his friends. They never hurt anyone, they were good people, my brother he was a good person." She babbled, tears still spilling from behind the lenses of her glasses.

"I'm so sorry, I can't explain it..."

"Bullshit!" Agnes spat, "You led my brother and friends to their deaths! Led them like lambs to the slaughter! How could you even contemplate such a thing?"

"I...I..." Dawn sighed, returning to the zipper knowing her words meant nothing.

"Is that all you have to say for yourself?"

Dawn said nothing, but focused on untangling the material from the zipper.

"As far as I'm concerned their blood is on your hands!"

"You're right." Dawn sighed, finally fixing her zip and handing the bag back to her.

"You're poison." Agnes said, shaking her head as Dawn turned away to focus on some old photographs of places and people from Maple Falls' past that hung from the wall next to the booth. She focused on an image of Beau Tooth and all his old hunting buddies, only Chopper Hardwood was still alive from that group now, each one had perished at the hands of Beau Tooth. Her finger tips slid over a smiling man with dark hair and a moustache above his pearly whites.

"No, I'm not poison." Dawn said absently.

"Then what would you call it?"

"I did what I did, out of some misguided act of morality."

Agnes laughed at that, it was a mocking sound that echoed around the diner and Dawn didn't care for it.

"I said it was misguided, didn't I?" Dawn snapped as she turned around to face her.

"Misguided is the understatement of the year!"

"I lost the love of my life to that monster." Dawn growled.

Agnes' eyes grew saucers, magnified even more by her spectacles.

"When they found that cabin covered in blood and those girls were missing a search party was sent out to find them."

"Girls? What girls? I don't know what you're talking about?"

Dawn stood up and approached the table where Agnes had retreated and found a chair and sat on it, rubbing at her temples, she did so hate reliving such trauma.

"Tooth killed his wife and daughters in that cabin, the same cabin where your brother and his friends lost their lives." She swallowed hard, Agnes was right, she knew, she was just as much to blame for this as Tooth was, in many ways she continued to fuel the beast's perverse crusade.

"How old were they? The girls, were they young?" Agnes asked gently.

"Charlotte was 8. Abigail was only 5 and she was suffering with leukaemia."

"Jesus!" Agnes gasped, a hand instinctively moving up to cover her mouth.

"He mounted their heads on the wall of the cabin and was never seen again."

Agnes tried to find words but there were none.

"I lost my own true love because of all this. My Reggie." Tears began to gather on Dawn's lower eyelashes and when she blinked they fell freely. She let them fall and continued to talk.

"Reggie was part of the search party that was sent to find Tooth. They never did and Reggie never came home. They found his rifle and his cap, but I never saw him again. I guess he was Tooth's first victim, after his poor family of course."

Agnes nodded and reluctantly, her hand slid across the table and found its way onto Dawn's. She was embarrassed for her reaction, that she had not taken into account that others had been affected by this monster, Beau Tooth. That she was the only person that it had affected was arrogant and ignorant and she knew it. She felt her face glow with shame.

"I'm sorry...for your loss." Agnes said gently, it was a halfhearted apology for her behaviour, as well as the vicious slap, but she couldn't bring herself to lose her ego and that was as good an apology as Dawn was going to get at this time.

Dawn smiled, she could read between the lines, but truly she knew that she didn't deserve an apology.

"I just couldn't put myself through that again, I couldn't put the town through it again. It was horrible I know and it was a heinous act, but it was meant with good intentions, so that people of this town didn't have to suffer like I was made to suffer. I did what I did year in and year out to save my friends. Even though we still lost some of them over the years due to their own stupidity more than anything. Those that didn't heed

154

the warnings fell to his axe. I just tried to do what I thought was best."

"I understand." Agnes nodded, and she did, even though it was a horrible act, she understood why and that was all she needed to know.

"I'm sorry your brother was one of those taken, I truly am." Dawn said to Agnes, placing her hand on top of hers and squeezed it tightly.

Agnes smiled and nodded.

"I just fear for us now." Dawn sighed.

"Why now?"

"If there are no pawns left on the board then the game changes."

"What do you mean?"

"There are no lambs that have been led this year. No victims to satisfy his bloodlust."

Agnes's eyes doubled again, her pupils quivering with moisture and horror as she gasped.

"He'll come here!"

Dawn nodded and dropped her head, a part of her knew that this was the end.

Suddenly there was a sound of raised voices from outside, the pair instinctively turned to face the window, but it was dark outside and the streetlights reflected off the snow and against the glass making it difficult to see anything.

"What is going on out there?" Agnes asked, standing up as Dawn looked up to the heavens and tears fell again.

"He's here." She whispered.

The body of a man came hurtling through the diner's window and collided with tables and chairs as Agnes stumbled backwards and Dawn stood up to catch her. The pair held each other as the body of a man twitched frantically.

"Jacques!" Dawn gasped in horror.

His whole body protruded with shards of glass, arteries were severed and they spurted out blood in all directions as he writhed around on the floor helplessly.

She couldn't believe her eyes, the death and terror was suddenly on her doorstep. This was Jacques Raymond, a frequent customer to the diner, every day he would order scrambled eggs, two rashers of bacon (very well done) and smother it in syrup. Now he squirmed on her floor as though he were making some sadistic snow angel in broken glass and blood.

And through the broken glass that clung to the window's jamb stood Beau Tooth, axe hanging by his side and a smile quivering across his lips, framed by the broken shards of glass like he was poised in the mouth of some demon. He stepped through snow and broken glass as he entered through the window and stepped into the diner. He dropped the axehead with a vicious strike, down into the face of the writhing man to put him out of his misery, before swivelling the axe in his hand and tasting the warmth of the fresh blood from its bit with his tongue. His eyes were wide and deranged and Agnes and Dawn held each other tighter still and screamed, for it was all they could think to do.

CHAPTER 18

Sheriff Russell burst through the shrubs of Maple Woods, disrupting the settled snow and sending it into a frenzy, it exploded in his face and refreshed him as he continued to follow the sledge tracks at speed. He slipped and was sent tumbling into the snow several times, but on each occasion he picked himself up and continued on his way. Determination forced him to keep going and the hope that he could reach the town before Beau Tooth. Several times he had tried to reach the office but he had had no success, deep down knowing that at certain points in the woods the lines of communication were not great and the gigantic sentinels that reached up and pierced the darkening sky interfered with the radio transmissions. He stopped at a clearing, taking a moment to catch his breath and regroup, he needed to gather his wits and calculate where he actually was.

He found that he was lagging and the sprint through the woods had taken its toll on him.

"I need to start exercising." He gasped, hands on his thighs as he spat into the snow. Steam rose from his clammy neck and for a moment he no longer felt the cold, but he did feel sick with what could be happening back in town. He stood up and breathed out slowly and gazed around the clearing, it was obvious that the sledge had spent some time stationed here and then moved off through the woods towards the road.

It was becoming more difficult to see as the sun had all but disappeared, leaving only the darkness of the surrounding woods and the paleness of the snow covered floor.

He removed his flashlight and activated it, a beam of light lit the clearing more than he had expected and for a moment he squinted from its brightness as it collided with the snow.

"Raymond, come in. Do you copy over?"

Again he tried the radio transmitter and all he could hear was static, there was the slight sound of Deputy Clegg's voice that flitted in and out but his words were broken and incomprehensible.

"I need a heavy presence in town, I repeat, heavy presence. Beau Tooth is real! I repeat, is real and is headed into town."

A scramble of static spat back at him.

"Blast." Growled Sheriff Russell as he slid the receiver back into position on its patch of velcro that hung from his parka.

"I hope he could hear me at least."
He let the beam of the flashlight swoop around the clearing and suddenly it picked something out in the whiteness of fallen snow.

"What's that?" He said to himself, moving closer to the object half buried in the snow and glittering back at him. He stooped down and saw a shard of silver protruding out from the snow. He retrieved it knowing exactly what it was as soon as his cold hands touched it.

"Oh, no..." He murmured, wiping away snow from the badge of the Maple Falls Sheriff Office, blood underneath smeared across the red maple leaf that was etched into the design giving the illusion that it was bleeding. It turned the snow pink and he wiped the excess onto his pants.

"Nate." He grimaced, the badge belonged to his Sergeant, Nathan Brown and knew that it was too late to save him. He held the badge in his palm for a moment, squeezing it tightly as he stood up. He turned the badge around and saw a piece of office issue parka material still attached to the safety pin that would have held it in place.

"You left this here on purpose, didn't you Nate?"

He nodded and slipped it into his pocket.

"A true Sergeant until the end." He sighed.

He noticed that the sledge tracks would lead him back through the heavy cover of woods and then reach the road further on. He gazed around and could just make out the crooked shelter that belonged to Eddie Gotch.

"Gotch's place." He declared, now finally knowing exactly where he was.

He knew that if he headed for the shack he would come out on Maple Cross and if he headed back down that road he would find his 4x4 waiting for him, which would make for a swifter return.

As he quickly trudged through the snow towards Gotch's shack someone or something moved in front of him, a quick movement that swept through the beam of his flashlight.

"Hello!" He called instinctively, a part of him hoping that it would be Sergeant Brown and that he was still alive.

He quickened his pace once more, running on adrenaline now more than anything and drew closer to the shack, shining the flashlight all around the seemingly deserted structure.

"Anybody there?" He called as he reached it.

There seemed like there was nothing and there were no tracks in the snow, any tracks that had been made by

Sergeant Brown had been covered already by the constant falling of snow.

"Hello? Is there anybody there?" He called again but there was no response. He started to think that maybe it was just some creature fleeing from him and stepped onto the road where Sergeant Brown's squad car was sitting idly, its windshield smashed, tyres shredded to nothing but flayed pieces of rubber and the light bars fitted to the roof were shattered.

"There's Nate's car. Tooth really did a number on it."

Out of the corner of his eye he saw movement and the broken door to Gotch's shack screeched as it rocked back and forth on what hinges remained.

"Mr Gotch?" He called, "Eddie, is that you?"

There was again no reply but there was the sound of a scuffle coming from within.

Sheriff Russell lay the shotgun down on the hood of Sergeant Brown's 4x4 and unclipped his revolver, he did this as he needed to use the flashlight and he couldn't juggle the shotgun and the flashlight at the same time.

"This is Sheriff Russell." He called edging closer to the door, flashlight and revolver gripped in each hand, crossed at the wrists, both pieces of equipment leading the way.

"Eddie, if you're in here you'd better let me know."

Still there was no answer and with a quickening pulse and a deep breath he kicked open the door on to the empty shack that had been demolished. It sat in total darkness and as he let the flashlight beam explore the inside of the shack, he saw what disarray it was in.

The beam met two dark marbles shimmering in the light of the torch, moist and scared, a whining sound emitting from them.

"Nora?" He whispered and knelt down for a better look and there curled up and shivering was Eddie Gotch's pet sheepdog, Nora.

"Nora, c'mon girl, c'mon now." He said calmly.

She slid her nose out from underneath the armchair, her face one of confusion and fear, her whole body shivered and her tail was coiled up between her legs as she approached him with great caution.

"Come girl, it's me, your old pal, Patrick." He smiled and shone the light up at his face, "You remember me, girl?"

Nora came to him eagerly and was grateful for the contact, it calmed her when he stroked her and cuddled her.

"We gotta get back to town, Nora. I think I will have to deputise you." He gazed into her dark eyes, "Are you up for the task, Deputy?"

Nora barked and wagged her tail excitedly.

"Come on then."

He ran past Brown's squad car, retrieved his shotgun and headed down the road towards where he had parked, it was a way to go, but Nora stuck with him all the way.

CHAPTER 19

It was as if time stood still when Beau Tooth heaved his massive bulk through the broken shards that was once the window of *Dawn's Diner*. Agnes and Dawn stood quivering, holding each other with matching gaping maws of distress. Both of them feeling exactly the same confusion, distress and fear. And it was the fear that held them there on the linoleum, toes curled up inside their shoes, toenails scraping at their insoles. Fear had frozen them where they stood and it was as though not even a bulldozer could have prised them from that very spot.

The sound of Tooth's boots cracking the broken shards of glass underfoot was all that could be heard, a haunting sound that grew nearer, slowly as if he were stalking his prey, he could take his time for they did not move, they did not even attempt to escape. Tooth cared not, he would take the offering and continue on his way, these people standing in front of him meant nothing to him, people in general meant nothing to him, all he had in his life was the need to survive.

"B-Beau..." Dawn spluttered, tears rolling down her face, the word trickled from her lips like a hiss and for a moment it halted the axe wielding behemoth in his tracks. His heavy boots still topped with melting snow came to a halt, treading down hard on a particularly large piece of glass, splitting it in two with a loud cracking sound as he stared down at the pair.

"B-Beau...it's me. It's Dawn." She said manoeuvring herself in front of Agnes in a feeble attempt to shield her from him.

"Dawn? What are you doing?" Agnes said, almost struggling from Dawn's forceful movements. Agnes' instinct was to face this together, Dawn's was that of a motherly instinct and to protect the young.

"Just stay behind me!"

"But..."

"But nothing!" Dawn snapped, "This is my mess and I will take the medicine. You on the other hand have got to get out of here."

Beau Tooth's eyes flitted from side to side at the two women, but he did nothing, it looked as though he wanted them to run or fight or do something, just to make this game of his worth while.

"Beau!" Dawn cried, the sound was strong and forceful and that got his attention. It had been many years since anyone had been so aggressive towards him that he had forgotten what it felt like. It must have triggered something in him from his past, growing up, a voice of authority that scolded him, a parent or teacher perhaps, whatever it was caused his scarred brow to ripple with an unpleasant scowl and he flung the axe up to meet his other hand and cradle it as if preparing to split the quivering pair in half.

"BEAU!" Dawn spat, "That's your name! I remember it, even if you don't. Beau!"

Tooth seemed to take the time to ponder this and his gaze looked up above him at the flickering strip light that hung above his head, it was bright and almost blinding. He squinted against its brightness, he had become so accustomed to living in gloom and darkness that he felt as though the bright light was a blade piercing his skull and splitting his brain. He did not enjoy it, but still he gazed into it, to perhaps feel something, even if it was uncomfortable, even if it hurt. Perhaps the name meant something to him and he was searching for its meaning somewhere, about where he had come from and what he had gone through. Whatever was going through his head it gave Dawn time to react and she stooped down and retrieved a shard of broken glass.

"RUN!" She screamed at Agnes and pushed her out of reach of the beast, the push was forceful and it knocked her off her feet and she slid across the linoleum and glass.

The sound of Dawn's screams tore Tooth away from his revery, he growled and scowled, for a moment he could not see from the brightness of the strip light, flashing orbs of light floated in front of his face and he swiped at them instinctively like some animal. He swung the axe into the air and shattered the lights above his head, leaving only a few in the corners of the diner to light it.

"Agnes, I said run!" Dawn called again, spying the young girl sitting on the floor, shaking off the effects of the impact and trying to dig glass out of her legs.

It seemed to be a mistake by Dawn to give away Agnes's whereabouts and Beau Tooth turned his attention to the youngster, spinning the axe in his hands as the glowing orbs started to dissolve with each rapid blink of his eyes.

"No!" Dawn growled, "Not her! Me! Me you bastard, it's me you want. I'm to blame. Take me!"

Dawn launched herself toward him and drove the shard of glass into his thick back, it seemed to take all the effort she had to pierce what felt like several layers of flesh before it lodged in his spine, grinding on his ribcage and splintering. He growled in pain and instinctively swatted Dawn away with his arm, she was sent hurtling over a table and she too hit the ground hard onto a bed of broken glass.

"Dawn!" Agnes cried and scrambled frantically to get to her feet, using the counter to help her. She stood in two minds of what to do next, a part of her screamed at her to make for the door, head up the high street and get in the nearest vehicle going south that she could find and just get the hell out of town. But there was another part to her which pleaded with her to save Dawn.

Agnes watched on as Beau Tooth struggled to retrieve the shard of glass from his back, it was in such a position that he could not seem to reach it. She turned to Dawn, who was dragging herself up and their eyes met and Dawn smiled at her and mouthed the word 'Go'. Agnes' ears seemed to hear nothing now as though she were in a daze. The fall had caused her to bang her head and all there was, was a strange buzzing sound in her head like radio static.

"I can't leave you." Agnes cried back and made a step towards her, everything seemed to slow down, she could see Dawn's lips moving but couldn't make out what she was saying then time sped up way too fast as Beau Tooth was back and slammed a boot into Agnes' stomach that sent her sprawling back into the counter. Her hip and stomach both reeling from the effects of such a sudden impact and the air left her body as she gasped from the impact.

Tooth held the axe in one hand and a bloody shard in the other, he snapped the piece of glass in his blackened fingers and allowed it to drop to the floor.

"Get the hell out of here, Agnes. Please!" Dawn pleaded.

Agnes did not know what to do until she saw the axe head of Beau Tooth's shimmering from the flickering strip light and her life flashed before her eyes as it hurtled towards her. Dawn arrived to push her out of the way as the axe came down and splintered its way through the counter. Agnes fell towards the broken window and the bloodied corpse of Jacques Raymond who would never eat scrambled eggs again. Dawn skidded on the glass as she rose to her feet with more shards of glass in her hands and slammed them repeatedly into Beau Tooth's wide back as he struggled to retrieve his axe that was wedged in the broken counter. Agnes scrambled away on her backside from the blood-soaked corpse, sickened by the sight of his major artery in his neck still squirting out clots of blood. But still she couldn't bring herself to leave, she couldn't leave Dawn. The same part of her that told her to run, told her to leave Dawn, that she deserved everything she got for allowing this all to happen in the first place, but she had stopped listening to that voice.

Beau turned and gripped Dawn by the throat and lifted her off the floor, she gagged and choked, immediately dropping the shards of glass that dripped with the fresh crimson of Beau Tooth's wounds. He was about to rip her throat out when Agnes slammed a chair into his back, he didn't seem to acknowledge the first blow as if he were some bloodthirsty dog with his jaws locked on to his victims flesh. The Third blow hit home and split the flesh around the back of his head and he dropped Dawn to the ground and turned angrily to face Agnes who stood with the metal chair in her hands, the legs and backrest all twisted from the blows.

"Leave her alone you asshole!" Agnes squealed and launched the chair at him, but there was nothing behind the throw and it ricocheted off his chest and fell to the floor where he kicked it viciously out of the way. He gripped the handle of the axe again in two hands and headed towards her, swiping it at her and slamming it down on the floor, hoping each one would be the killing blow, but Agnes managed to evade each strike and all he did was cut through tables and booths. Dawn was back again slamming useless fists onto his back that did nothing but act as an annoyance to him, like some irritating fly buzzing around him. He grabbed her by the hair and threw her across the counter where she hit the back wall of shelves, homing all manner of coffee and tea bags, jars and cups and sent it all hurtling on top of her as she fell broken behind the counter.

171

Tooth again turned his attention to Agnes and this time he moved with purpose across the diner towards her, turning over tables and kicking away chairs that were in his way. Agnes found herself throwing all manner of condiments at him because it was all she could find, but it did nothing but amuse him. By the time she tried to reach for her rucksack it was too late and he grabbed her by her hair and lifted her into the air, before slamming her down through a table with such force that she must have blacked out for a moment because when she came too he was leaning over her with his massive hand around her throat, squeezing tightly. She gagged and choked, she could not seem to get any air into her lungs and she could feel her face throbbing as if it might explode at any second.

"Leave her alone!" Came the shriek and again Dawn was somehow on her feet, her body twisted, her arm limp as if broken and useless, blood trickled down her forehead and face from an unseen wound deep in her mass of dishevelled hair and she limped out on a broken ankle from behind the counter. She slammed a cutlery drawer on part of the countertop that still stood and retrieved a huge kitchen knife.

"I have told you it's me you want. Not her, now let her go."

With those words lingering in the air and Agnes on the verge of passing out forever, the kitchen knife was

172

launched and sunk into Beau Tooth's back. He grimaced and cried out, letting go of his grip on Agnes and letting her collapse into a heap, gasping for that much needed air.

He reached around and found the handle of the knife and slid it out of yet another wound deep in his back and discarded the knife making straight for Dawn with speed this time.

"You bastard, Beau. You need to die! You must!" Dawn shrieked as she launched utensil after utensil at him, most of them bounced off him never even stopping his momentum. Knives of all different shapes and sizes cut the air and slid past him, missing their target, some hit home and stuck in his thick flesh but did little to stop his approach and he was at her again with a hand grabbing at her face and throat. Tearing and ripping the flesh away as she screamed, blood seeping through his fingers and down her waitress uniform staining it crimson, the blood flow unstoppable like a broken faucet.

There was a loud gunshot and a bullet whisked through the air and slid straight through Tooth's shoulder. He groaned and immediately released Dawn's broken body that fell into the wreckage of her broken counter, motionless. He spun around favouring his shoulder to see Old Sparky standing in the craggy maw of the broken window with a rifle in hand.

"C'mon Miss. It's time you left." Old Sparky said to Agnes, who gazed at the lifeless body of Dawn and with tears in her eyes she staggered to her feet and clutched her rucksack to her chest.

"But...Dawn."

"Ain't nothing you can do for her now, Miss. Now go on, get!"

Agnes made her escape spilling out onto the snow covered high street.

Old Sparky gazed at a man that he used to know and scowled, chewing eagerly on a curd of tobacco and spat it onto the floor.

"Now you get your ugly ass outta this diner, Tooth. Good people gotta eat here." He spat again and aimed the rifle at his target, closing one eye to take aim.

"And you ain't good people."

He let loose a second bullet that hurtled through the air towards Beau Tooth.

CHAPTER 20

Lieutenant Tammy Adams strolled into the Maple Falls Sheriff Office ready for the long twelve hours that awaited her. She yawned and then sighed, the night shift was always slow going in Maple Falls, unless there was a drunken ruckus that had broken out at *Chopper's,* there was rarely anything to do. Which suited her, it usually meant that she would either use the time to reorganise the files or read a good book, or sometimes a bad book, anything to pass the time would do. She stood in the reception area yawning loudly, she had tried to sleep at home but had only managed a few hours, she found it very difficult to sleep during the day especially when she had things on her mind. The morning spent with Agnes had played on her mind, she felt for the girl and was saddened that they couldn't help her. She knew as well as anybody that the chances of her brother being found alive now were slim to none. She approached the desk and behind it Deputy Clegg sat at the radio transmitter, thick with sweat, so much so that it seeped through the beige coloured shirt and made patches that looked brown.

Lieutenant Adams frowned as she took in this strange scene, he looked very flustered by something, almost scared. Deputy Clegg was never really good under pressure and if truth be told had no business in the role of Deputy, but he was just the next one on the ladder and it filled a hole at the time. But as time passed it was quite obvious to everyone concerned that he was a round peg in a square hole. Sheriff Russell knew the concerns but didn't have the heart to demote him. Lately Sheriff Russell hadn't cared about much that was going on around the office and Lieutenant Adams had had to take the reins and pick up the slack. But Tammy Adams didn't mind, she would do anything for Sheriff Russell, but tonight she found herself very concerned as Deputy Clegg looked close to tears and was constantly trying to reach someone on the radio.

"Raymond?" She asked, leaning on the desk.

He turned around on his swivel chair, eyes almost moist, he was visually flustered. She had seen him like this before when he was overwhelmed.

"Whatever is the matter?"

"Oh, Tammy, thank goodness you're here."

"What is it? You look so pale, are you unwell?"

"No, yes..." he spluttered, dabbing away the sweat from his brow with the back of his hand, "...I don't know."

"Just calm down. You're not making any sense." Adams' tone was calming and motherly as was her instincts.

She moved around the desk and approached him, crouching in front of him and holding his hand.

"I don't know what to do, I just don't know what to do, Tammy."

"Hush, now take your time and tell me what's wrong. I can't help you if you don't tell me, Raymond." Deputy Clegg nodded and took a few deep breaths, they were shaky at first and they fluttered in his throat struggling to escape, but after a few moments he seemed to calm.

"Now, what is it?" She asked.

"I received a frantic message from Sheriff Russell, broken words I couldn't piece together to make sense of and now I can't seem to reach him at all."

"It's okay, he's probably just in a patch of the woods that has a bad connection. I take it, that's where he is again?"

Clegg nodded.

"But, he mentioned Beau Tooth and dead and blood and I don't know what else, just words and none of them were good."

177

"Perhaps send Nate out there and see if he can track him down."

Clegg shook his head and his bottom lip trembled.

"I can't reach Nate either, he went out hours ago to check on Eddie Gotch and now nothing."

"That's not like Nate?" Tammy looked at her watch and realised that his shift should have ended an hour ago.

"I know, I just don't know what to do, it's all getting too much for me."

Clegg groaned and tears started to form in his eyes.

"Okay Raymond, there's no need to get upset, we'll sort it out. You'll see."

Clegg nodded and stood up from the chair, he was unsteady on his feet and swayed from side to side.

"Go and get yourself a coffee and try Nate's cell phone."

"Okay, Tammy." Clegg said with a sigh, relieved to get away from the radio and its nasty spitting of static. He disappeared into the staff room as Lieutenant Adams slid into the seat and tried both Sergeant Brown and Sheriff Russell on the radio, but there was no response.

Tammy sat back in her seat and pondered the words that Raymond had mentioned.

Beau Tooth. Dead. Blood.

"Could mean a number of things." She said to herself and changed the frequency on the radio transmitter, knowing her way around the job better than her Deputy did. She knew that sometimes you had to go through all the channels to sometimes get the right frequency, especially this time of year when the snow started to fall, it always played havoc with the radio connection.

The radio spat and crackled and there was the faint crackle of Sheriff Russell's voice.

"Gotcha!" Tammy cried and turned it back to where she had heard her superior's voice. Suddenly his voice came through loud and clear, he was flustered and by the roar of a car engine he was driving at speed.

"Sheriff!" Tammy cried, "Where are you? What's going on?"

"It's all about to kick off, Tammy."

"What do you mean? We've lost contact with Nate too and Raymond has been a wreck..."

"Nate is dead." Came the groan on the other end of the radio transmitter.

"What?" Tammy gasped and leaned back in her seat with her hand over her mouth as Deputy Clegg arrived and on hearing the words dropped the two mugs of coffee onto the floor. They smashed and erupted with hot black liquid across the floor as he stood gaping.

179

"Nate's d-dead?" He murmured.

Tammy turned to him and her eyes were moist and full of sympathy.

"I can't explain everything now, I'm on my way back, I'm already riding my luck with the road, it's treacherous!"

"I don't understand what's happening?" Tammy said.

"Everything I said was true and we've got to stop him."

"Who?" Tammy asked

"Tooth. He's real, he's alive and he's heading for town.

"Good God! Tammy gasped.

"For all I know he's already there."

"W-what do we do?" Raymond snivelled, tears falling from his eyes for the loss of his good friend and colleague.

"Get everyone you can into town asap! Lives might just depend on it. Over and out!"

The Sheriff's voice had gone and was replaced with static.

"T-Tammy what are we going to do?" He stood in a puddle of coffee, his hands held out as if he were still gripping the handles of the mugs, his fingers quivering.

Tammy rose from the seat and approached him, she hugged him.

"I know this is a huge shock and I know Nate was your friend. But we need to focus. There is some serious shit going down and we need to act."

"But..."

"I know, I know. We will have to grieve later but the safety of the town takes priority."

"I know." He sighed and his head dropped and his eyes focussed on the puddle around his boots.

"Shall I get the mop?" He asked, almost ghostlike and automatic, robotic even.

"Leave the coffee, Raymond. We need to get every available officer out on the high street now."

"There's only us on shift."

"I'll contact them. They'll come in, don't worry. This is an emergency."

"What should I do?" Raymond asked

"Fuel up the Bobcat's and get up to the high street as soon as you can."

He breathed in and nodded before heading out the door. Tammy watched him leave and dialled the first officer and couldn't help but thinking that was the last time she was going to see Raymond Clegg alive.

"I hope he's in the right frame of mind." She said to herself as her cell phone rang out unanswered.

CHAPTER 21

Several gunshots rang out from the diner as Agnes scrambled across the snow covered road, she turned on hearing the final gunshot and hoped that it would be the last. She hoped that the bullet had been the one to put an end to the monster. She stood in the middle of the high street staring at the diner, the broken maw of the front window appearing dark and menacing like the entrance to some curious cave.

She saw no movement and all that met her eyes was gloom framed with the gentle caress of thick flakes of white.

A strip light inside flickered for a moment and then stopped but it revealed nothing from that darkness within. There was an eerie silence that chilled her to the bone and she wrapped her arms around herself as if this gesture would again act as protection from what waited within. She noticed that at the sound of the gunshots, several lights of apartments that sat above shops sprang into life and curtains twitched, but no one looked too eager to come outside and investigate what was going on, and why would they?

"Mister...Sparky?" Agnes called, her fearful tones seemed to catch in her throat and sound more like a croak.

There was no answer from within and she called him again, this time with more authority but panicked, as a tear ran down her plump bruised cheek.

Suddenly there was a sound that escaped the diner, the sound of shuffling feet through shards of glass. Old Sparky came waddling through the broken window with his rifle in his hands, his fingers seemed anxious and wriggled around blindly at the trigger and the fore-stock, moving like spiders erratically wriggling to escape from something.

"Mister Sparky!" Agnes sighed with relief and she smiled, the old man exiting the diner first and alive meant that he had slain that gruesome bastard.

His boots broke glass and slid through snow as he staggered towards her, almost dreamlike were his movements, his head seemed to bow forward and rest on his chest, he looked to Agnes as though he was sleepwalking.

"Mister Sparky, did you get him? Please tell me you got him?" Agnes asked and took a step forward to meet him.

He finally came to a halt, his fingers still wriggling wildly with the rifle in his hands, an index finger finding the trigger and tugging on it several times, but the rifle stayed calm and didn't react by unloading its rounds. Perhaps it was empty or the rifle had jammed, either way Agnes was pleased as the way he was holding the gun he could have easily shot her where she stood.

"Is everything okay? Did you get him?"
Agnes' eyes were leaking again, it was uncontrollable, she couldn't seem to help it anymore.

"Please! Mister Sparky talk to me!"
He lifted his head and it seemed like so much effort for him, his face was gaunt and long with shock, his eyes were wide and full of fear.

"No." Agnes whispered, she knew by the look on his face that he was a dead man walking.
He spluttered incoherent words that made no sense to her and then there were no words that ran off his tongue, only thick wads of blood that gurgled in his throat before escaping down his chin like lava oozing from the mouth of a freshly erupted volcano.
He dropped the rifle into the snow at his feet and it went off causing Agnes to jump and almost fall backwards in the snow. The bullet whistled across the surface of the snow and cut through a car tyre that saw

it immediately flatten and set off the vehicle's whining alarm.

The rifle had in fact become jammed at obviously the wrong time and Old Sparky had paid the ultimate price. His neck could not seem to hold up the weight of his head and was whipped forwards way too far, his chin landing on his stomach as Agnes watched on in horror and clapped a hand over her mouth to either stifle a cry or halt the immediate flow of vomit that seemed inevitable.

With his body so bent forwards his spinal cord could be seen protruding out and upwards as he seemed to defy gravity by remaining on his feet, the top of his body leaned towards the ground before finally he fell face down in the snow. The impact caused his spinal cord to quiver from side to side frantically, sending plasma flicking into the air and landing in clumps in the snow, its heat causing it to immediately melt and steam rise up from the craters.

"Good God, no..." Agnes managed before the vomit came and hit the snow.

The sound of crunching glass met her ears again and sobered her up from her sickness and she stared at that window, hoping and praying that Dawn would come staggering out and not that bloodthirsty behemoth.

Her heart sank and her gut churned and knotted when Beau Tooth came into view. He lowered the axe and let the head collide with the floor and dragged it through the broken glass on his way towards the fallen carcass of Old Sparky that lay steaming in the snow.

The sadistic, playful smile that had caressed Beau Tooth's cleft palate earlier was gone and had been replaced with a serious sneer with saliva bubbling up and frothing through his broken teeth. His huge torso was bleeding in places where he had been struck by some of Old Sparky's bullets, some of them digging through the layers of human skin he wore as protection from the elements. But whatever injuries he was carrying, whatever discomfort or pain that he was feeling, it did not show and he bounded out of the diner and onto the snow covered street, striding towards Agnes.

Agnes screamed and backed off before bumping into Tooth's sleigh behind her. She turned round and saw the twisted frozen corpses that were left prone in it and screamed again staggering away from it. The car alarm still sang out and created an unattractive cacophony with her shrieks as Tooth strode past Old Sparky and reached down to pick him up by the spine. He didn't miss a stride and hoisted the carcass of the dead man up in the air as he moved towards Agnes and the sledge. Old Sparky swung from side to side, his limbs lifeless, being carried like a businessman would carry his briefcase.

Agnes backed away and ran, slipped up and landed in the snow, turning frantically believing that when she turned that he would be on her. But he was hoisting Old Sparky up by his spinal cord and throwing him unceremoniously onto the sledge. He looked at her and grinned before returning back to the diner.

Agnes took the moment to think, she couldn't understand why she was being spared, then it dawned on her when she saw Beau Tooth carrying the broken body of Jacques Raymond who came hurtling through the diner window only several minutes ago, which now felt like a lifetime to her. She slid backwards in the snow, trying to clamber to her feet and turn away to make a run for it until she heard the sound of Jacques Raymond joining Old Sparky and the others in the sledge. She knew now that it was her turn and slowly turned around to face him, her chest heaving heavily and her breath escaping in a plume of warmth to cut through the falling freezing snow. He stood staring at her with the axe cradled in his hands, he spun it playfully allowing the streetlights to collide with the steel head and the thick wads of flesh and blood that clung to it.

"Fuck you!" Agnes cried and stood defiantly.

She knew now that her brother was dead, that there was no way of coming face to face with this monster and surviving. She wondered if her brother had been

187

brave like she had been in his final moments or if he didn't know it was coming then at least he would not feel the fear that was flowing through her body right now.

"I love you, Quack." She whispered and clenched her fists and hoped for a swift ending.

But all she heard was Tooth's heavy footsteps through the snow as he returned once again to the diner.

"Dawn!" She gasped with realisation, "He's going back for Dawn."

Agnes didn't know why she felt the need to do what she did next, that voice in her head was telling her to get the hell out of there, anywhere away from this beast. She was a fool to still be standing there, two times Tooth had given her a free pass, not to survive but to at least make an attempt at an escape.

"You silly bitch," She said to herself stooping down into the snow and forming a ball of snow with her hands, "What the hell are you doing?"

Agnes stood and launched the snowball through the air and it collided with the bald scarred head of Beau Tooth.

"Boo ya!" Agnes yelped, with a ridiculous smile on her face that immediately fell as she swallowed hard.

Tooth span on the spot, his boots kicked up a cloud of snow and his face was red with anger. He growled, it was such a sound that it was heard over the bellowing of the car alarm and he bounded towards her, leaving the broken body of Dawn Rougeau as nothing but an afterthought.

"For fuck's sake!" Came a cry from further down the high street and the angry growl caused both Beau Tooth and Agnes to turn in the direction of the blaring car alarm.

A rotund woman with her hair in curlers and wrapped in a housecoat clambered across the sidewalk towards the red Volkswagen Beetle. Her round face glowed with annoyance as she used her key fob to turn off the alarm.

"Stupid thing!" She spat as she surveyed the car, "Been pressing the Goddamn thing for ten minutes, should fucking work, modern technology!"

The complaints of Gertrude Cassidy who was the proprietor of the town's sewing and alterations shop fell on deaf ears and it wasn't until Agnes saw that Beau Tooth was now marching down the high street towards her did she realise that she wasn't going to be the next victim after all.

Gertrude shuffled through the snow and found the punctured tyre and threw her arms up in the air and cursed the world again.

"Oh, just fucking great! Which one of these drunken, inbred jerks did this?"

She turned around and saw a man striding towards her, half hidden by a veil of falling snow.

"Oh, is this your doing?" She moaned and sneered at the silhouette approaching her.

"Oh, you mean business, do ya?" She scoffed and rolled up the sleeves of her housecoat to reveal thick forearms and clenched fists that were hefty and looked as though they could do damage.

"NO!" Agnes called, sounding the alarm but it was too late and by the time Beau Tooth stepped through the veil of snow and Gertrude could see him, the axe whistled through the air and took her head off in one action. It spun in the air and bounced on the roof of her beloved car and started the alarm off again. Instantly her hand twitched as if to activate the key fob as she stood headless with blood oozing out from her throat. She dropped the key fob into the snow and her hefty carcass soon followed it. Beau Tooth became enraged by the sound of the alarm and suddenly started to lay into the vehicle with reckless abandon, destroying it with the axe.

Finally the alarm conceded and Agnes ran to the nearest building which happened to be *Chopper's Bar* and she disappeared inside.

Gas started to leak out of the wreckage that once resembled a 1998 Volkswagen Beetle, and smoke had started to rise from its engine.

Tooth slammed the axe head into Gertrude's head and it bit into it and held it tightly allowing him to pick the axe up and carry her head as he grabbed the leg of the large woman and dragged her in the snow towards the sledge, the car caught fire and exploded behind him but he did not even miss a stride.

CHAPTER 22

Agnes Duckworth tumbled into *Chopper's Bar* and slammed the door behind her. Something in her rucksack crunched loudly as she fell up against the door, chest heaving, flesh clammy and pale, stomach churning. She knew immediately that the sound was her laptop screen shattering into a thousand pieces but paid it no mind, there were more important things going on than broken laptops. Her spectacles were fogged up by her own heavy breaths coming in from out of the cold but her ears could hear the sensuous tones of *Shania Twain* asking her to come on over. She quickly wiped away the fog from her spectacles and slid them back into place where she was met by a number of faces gawping back at her with bemusement.

Chopper and Wendy stood behind the bar looking a little concerned by her arrival and instinctively Wendy clasped Chopper's arm thinking the worst.

Other eyes that glared at her as she looked around seemed to judge her, she felt stupid for a moment and her skin burned with embarrassment as some shook their heads and went back to their drinks. It was not a busy night and there were only a handful of patrons, perhaps it was still too early in the evening, but there were some familiar faces there, ones she had seen in the bar from her first visit. The bunch of men playing cards that had been so aggressive and boorish towards Sheriff Russell.

"Are you staying or going?" Called Ike Rayburn, the loudmouthed one of the bunch, his trademark toothpick protruding from his thick black beard as he gnawed it angrily with his teeth.

"You lose, Ike." Laughed Ira clapping his hands together and clawing at the dollar bills on the table. Hank and Ben threw their cards down on the table in frustration but Ira glared at the girl slumped up against the door.

"Come on, Ike, pay up." Hank said, nudging him.

"What?" Ike snapped, "What is it?"

"You lost, big man." Ben laughed, "Now pay up."

"Yep! Time to pay the piper." Cackled Ira, "Now come on cough it up."

"Fuck this shit!" Ira growled, staring at his cards, "I had a winning hand."

"Then you should have played it." Hank shrugged.

"Fuck!" Ike growled and threw a twenty dollar bill towards the grinning face of Ira, "Choke on it you toothless old buzzard."

Ira chuckled and held the bill up to the light to check its authenticity and then chewed on it before slapping it down on his growing pile of winnings.

Ike chewed on his toothpick and stared at Agnes.

"If you'd have been paying attention you may well have won." Ben said, taking a swig of *Bobby's*.

"Yeah, instead of eyeing up that young doe over there." Ira laughed.

"Shut up and deal the cards." Ike growled.

"She looks distressed." Hank noticed.

"Yeah, that's how Ike likes 'em!" Laughed Ira.

"Shut the hell up." Ike snarled and picked at his teeth with the toothpick and smiled at Agnes who was straightening up her glasses and taking in the room. Her breaths were heavy and her bosom rose and fell underneath her parka. Ike licked at his lips.

"Although I wouldn't mind a bit of that."

"Jesus, Ike! Have you no boundaries?" Ben scoffed, "She's old enough to be your daughter."

"How fucking old do you think I am?" Ike snapped and scooped up his cards pretending to ignore the girl.

"Old enough to know better." Ira sniffed.

Agnes staggered into the bar, dazzled by the flashing lights of the jukebox and pinball machine.

"Are you okay, dear?" Wendy called from behind the bar, she gestured for her to approach them. Agnes's mouth moved but she couldn't find the words and she swayed from side to side as if at any moment she would collapse.

"He...He..." Agnes stuttered through congested breaths.

"What's she doing? Her best *Wacko Jacko* impression?" Hank sniggered.

The table laughed apart from Ike who reached out to grab her arm, perhaps to steady her, perhaps to make an inappropriate advance.

"Hey, girl..." Ike said, but before he could complete his sentence Agnes turned to him and threw up all over him. Ike let go of her arm and she fell backwards and Hank caught her.

"What the fuck!" Ike growled and stood up from his chair, kicking it backwards as vomit dripped into his beard.

The others laughed at his misfortune.

"Stupid bitch!" He growled and gestured to go for her.

"Sorry." Agnes murmured, not feeling as though she was really there, her head was a whirl from what she had just witnessed.

"Ike that's enough!" Chopper said, throwing him a towel.

"But the bitch hurled on me!" Ike cried, wiping it away quickly from his face with the towel.

Those around the table could not contain themselves and laughed until tears ran down their cheeks, after witnessing such a scene.

"Leave it." Chopper said, taking Agnes by the hand and leading her towards the bar.

"She needs a good slapping! That's what she needs." Ike continued, unable to let it go.

"I said leave it, Ike!" Chopper turned on the spot and his eyes were burning. Ike had never seen Chopper like that before, although he had heard of stories telling him to never trifle with Old Chopper. The look silenced him and he fell back into his chair and quietly emptied his bottle of beer.

"Are we playing cards or what?" He snarled, red with embarrassment as the others burst out laughing at him once more.

"What's the matter, dear? What's happened?" Chopper asked her as he propped her up against the bar, she instinctively slid onto a bar stool as she tried to shake away the cobwebs.

"Tell us what's happened, we can help." Wendy said reassuringly as she slid a glass of water towards her and patted her hand.

Agnes looked up at her with eyes wide, magnified by her glasses and shook her head.

"You can't help." She whispered.

"We can, can't we Chopper?" Wendy said with a smile.

"Of course we can." Chopper gave her a reassuring smile and put his hand on her shoulder.

"Whatever is wrong, whatever has happened we can help you fix it." Wendy reiterated and gave Agnes' hand a squeeze.

Agnes felt claustrophobic with them surrounding her and broke away, staggering away from them.

"You can't help. Nobody can help." She started to cry again.

"Will somebody shut that bitch up!" Ike called from the table.

"Quiet, Ike!" Wendy snapped, "Can't you see the girl is distraught!"

"See it?" Ike scoffed, "I can smell it!" And gestured to the vomit quickly drying on his shirt which caused the others to laugh again.

"SHUT UP!" Agnes cried and her high-pitched, frantic tone silenced the bar and all eyes were on her again.

"Settle down, dear." Wendy tried to calm her and approached her, but stopped in her tracks by Agnes holding her hand out towards her.

"No!" Agnes panted as if she were on the verge of a panic attack, "You can't help me. You can't help yourself, don't you understand? No one is safe. No one!"

"Safe from what?" Chopper asked, confusion wrinkling his balding head.

"He's here damn it! He's here!" She cried.

"Who's here?" Wendy asked.

"What's she prattling about?" Ike sighed.

"H-Him..." Agnes spluttered.

Chopper seemed to sense something and the white hairs on his thick tattooed forearms stood to attention and a cold chill ran through his veins.

"Beau Tooth." He whispered.

There was an explosion from out on the high street and orange and amber flashed behind the speckled glass of the windows. Everyone seemed to shake in their seats and then waited as still as statues for something, for anything to tell them that it wasn't their imagination. There was a second explosion and the glass of the windows rattled in its frames, the neon sign that advertised beer quivered and banged against the glass. Still in the background *Shania Twain* continued her song, as if she were trying to ease the tension.

"What the hell is going on out there?" Hank said and rose from his chair.

The door swung open and a bear of a man filled the frame as he stepped in, kicking snow from his boots as they thudded on the wooden floorboards of *Chopper's Bar*.

"Jesus!" Hank murmured as he fell back into his seat.

Beau Tooth gripped the axe tightly in his hands and his massive chest rose and fell with heavy breaths of expectancy, for he knew that he had a fight on his hands.

CHAPTER 23

The chained tyres of Sheriff Russell's Ford F150 Lariat tore into the crisp layer of fresh snow scrapping viciously on the frozen asphalt. At such ludicrous speeds, the chains sparked and the wheels that were held with their confines shuddered at the impact and threatened to spin off the road at any moment.

A thick layer of sweat cascaded down from underneath Sheriff Russell's ushanka hat as he gripped the steering wheel and bared his teeth.

"Come on, come on, don't you fail me now." He murmured to the Ford as if spurring on a flagging stallion as he rode it into the ground.

The headlights shone wildly, the colour of homemade lemonade, bright and alive, but through the darkness presented nothing new ahead but the whiteness of snow. As he hurtled back towards town a fresh flurry of snow fell and consumed him, making his job considerably difficult, his windshield wipers now brought into action to sweep away the falling snow, but it was a doomed task.

"Damn it!" He growled, "Fucking snow! I'm sick to the back teeth of the stuff."

A grumble and a whine trembled up from the floor of the passenger side and his eyes flitted to meet those of the terrified looking sheepdog nestled as far under the seat as it could get.

"It's okay Nora, it's okay girl." He said in a reassuring tone. The steering wheel momentarily slipped through his fingers and the vehicle shuddered almost losing its grip.

"Sheesh!" He cried and managed to gain control again with a deep exhale, "That was a close one."

Nora whined again and in her eyes he could see fear.

He wondered whether it was the dog's fear that he was seeing or his own manifested in the reflection of her eyes. He told himself that it was Nora that was scared and that was enough to get him by for another few hundred yards.

Still Nora whined at him, it's as if she were telling him to slow down or to stop altogether. But he paid her no mind and instead made fun of her discomfort.

"Stop your grumbling, Nora. You're like an old woman, with your constant whining. We'll soon be there, you'll see."

No sooner had the words left his lips that the chained tyres that had rid their luck for way too long failed and the car went skidding off the road.

It was all Sheriff Russell could do to hold onto the steering wheel and try to control the inevitable crash. The vehicle spun around and around, spraying the surrounding trees with the brightness of the headlights, shards of light cutting through the snow and trees in dizzying rotation like searchlights trailing an escaped convict.

Patrick Russell closed his eyes tightly, the spinning and the brightness of the headlights was all too much for him. He could hear Nora crying and the wheels cutting through the deep snow until the driver's side slammed into a tree and the motion came to an abrupt end.

He opened his eyes slowly and all he saw was white, snow covered the windshield and he breathed a sigh of relief that he was still in one piece.

"Looks like someone's looking out for me at least." He quipped and turned to Nora who was curled into a ball quivering, her dark eyes wide and glazed like marbles.

"You okay, girl?" He asked and smiled at her.

She whined and growled in reply as if chastising him for his recklessness.

"Okay, okay, fair enough. I hear ya."

He slapped his hand on the passenger's seat and gestured for Nora to join him. Her head tilted to one side and her ears flopped with the movement as she peeked out from her refuge under the seat and her dark eyes shone, asking for reassurance.

"It's okay. Come on."

Nora cautiously made her way onto the passenger seat and Sheriff Russell fussed her eagerly, stroking her head and neck and roughly behind the ears. Nora enjoyed it so much that she leapt onto his lap and began licking at his face.

"Okay, okay, calm down." He laughed, pushing her advances away but continuing to stroke her.

He looked out the driver's side window and all he could see was a wall of white, he attempted to open the door, but it would not open. He opened the window and some of the snow fell in on top of them, Nora yelped and retreated to the passenger seat once again.

"It's okay, it's just a bit of the white stuff, that's all."

As the window opened and the snow disappeared he realised that the door had become jammed due to the impact of a huge redwood. He touched the splintered bark of the tree next to him and he started the vehicle up once again and reversed as much as he could, the hood still submerged in a pile of snow.

"Looks like we're in a bit of a pickle." He said facing Nora, "How are you at digging?"

Unable to exit through the driver's side he leaned over and opened the passenger side allowing Nora to jump out which she did and scuttled off somewhere to do her business. Sheriff Russell dragged himself out over the seats and into the coldness of the night. He removed his hat and threw it back into the car, it may well be bitter out, but there was a thick sweat running down his spine that would keep him warm. He moved around to survey the vehicle, the front was covered in snow and he would have to remove that before he could be on his way. For a moment he pondered, could he leave the car and go out on foot? He wasn't too far away from town now, but decided that speed was needed here and he needed to conserve his energy for whatever horrors awaited him back in Maple Falls.

He retrieved a shovel from out of the trunk and when he slammed the trunk shut it echoed like a gun shot through the woods, the sound halted him in the snow and he listened as the echo seemed to carry on for far too long.

"If I didn't know better I'd say those were real gunshots." He pondered for a moment and pushed the thought to the back of his mind.

He gave a whistle and Nora came bounding through the snow, seemingly refreshed and no longer frightened.

"Don't think you're getting out of the hard work." He said, slamming the shovel into a pile of snow that gathered around the front of the car.

"Get digging!" He said and clicked his fingers and gestured with a point at the pile of snow. Nora replied with a playful bark and dived into it and began digging feverishly.

"Good girl." He said with a smile.

He grabbed his radio transmitter and spoke to headquarters, it seemed to take an age before there was finally an answer from a frantic Lieutenant Adams.

"Sheriff is that you?" She cried, her voice was flustered, normally calm under pressure and able to stay level headed. That scared Sheriff Russell, if Tammy Adams had been shook up, then all bets were off.

"Are you okay Tammy? You sound distraught!"

"I-I'm doing the... I'm okay, Sheriff, where are you?"

"Ive got stuck in the snow, gonna have to dig myself out, but I'm on my way. Anything to report?"

"Varying reports of sightings and disturbances on the high street."

"Of what exactly?"

"I couldn't say for sure. The callers were...scared. Or the lines went dead."

Sheriff Russell pondered that for a moment and hoped that wasn't a bad omen.

"Sheriff?" Came Tammy on the radio and she seemed distraught again, *"Patrick! Patrick, are you there?"*

"Yeah, I'm here. Sorry Tammy."

Tammy let out a sigh of relief.

"Do we have any officers at the scene?" The Sheriff asked.

"Deputy Clegg is leading the operation."

That didn't fill Sheriff Russell with confidence.

"I managed to reach Officer's Ouellett and Smith. They have both gone out on Bobcats. Officer Huffman is on a call to see Mrs Pascoe and Sergeant Church was asleep but she's on her way."

"Roger that, good work Tammy."

"I'm going to have to go too, Sheriff. I have to... they're going to need all the help they can get."

"No, Tammy you stay where you are, I need you there, that's an order."

Sheriff Russell knew that Tammy Adams was the heart and soul of that office and without her everything would go to shit. He couldn't even imagine life without her.

"But Sheriff, you know how big this is."

"I know and I will be there as soon as I can, but do not go out there, you hear me?"

There was an explosion from the town and Sheriff Russell nearly dropped the transmitter as snow was disturbed by the blast and sent it down upon him in a gentle flurry. Nora's head peeked out from the snow she was digging and whimpered.

"What the hell was that!" Sheriff Russell gasped and in the distance he could see a glow of orange flame and a rising plume of thick smoke.

"Tammy! Come in Tammy!"

"I'm here! Did you hear that?"

"What was it?"

"I don't know." Tammy sounded scared and she swallowed hard, *"I've got to go out there, I can't live with myself if I don't help them."*

"Tammy, no, stay where you are. That is a direct order!"

"Sorry. Lieutenant Adams out."

"Tammy? Tammy?" He screamed into the receiver but knew he would get no reply.

"Damn it!" He said and slapped the radio back into place on his parka.

There was a second explosion and he closed his eyes for a moment believing that this could well be the end of life in Maple Falls. He hopped to the job in hand and began to shovel frantically. Nora was still looking around, flustered by the loud explosions but when she gazed at Sheriff Russell and saw him eagerly digging at the heap of snow that buried the front of the car, she followed suit and began digging too.

207

CHAPTER 24

The patrons of Chopper's Bar seemed glued to their seats, fingers gripping the arms of the chairs so tightly that their fingernails left indentations in the wood. Eyes were wide in bewildered horror and mouths hung narrow and breathless at what stood before them, cradling a bloodstained axe.

Shania Twain had finished her cheerful country contralto and the vinyls shuffled inside the juke as the room sat in agonising silence.

The poker player table led by Ike Rayburn looked up from their hands, cards fanned out in front of them and eyebrows raised, immediately machismo seemed to take over and defensively their chests expanded.

A middle-aged man, known to all as Drunken Donald was slunk in a booth, a whiskey glass hanging at his lips, his drunken eyelids flickered, red and sore, he couldn't be sure that what he was seeing was even real. Could this sordid vision have been brought on by the eighth glass of whiskey he had consumed?

Nevertheless he watched on unmoving.

A young couple on a first date were sharing an ice cream sundae, leaning over it with eyes of lust for each other, but all that disintegrated at the arrival of this maniacal man beast.

The irony was not lost on the room as *Monty Python's* infamous *Lumberjack Song* burst into life causing all heads to turn in its direction. It even managed to grip Beau Tooth's attention as he turned towards the jukebox with indifference.

"Wendy, get her out of here!" Chopper said slowly reaching behind the bar and retrieving a baseball bat that was usually reserved for drunken louts that caused a ruckus on a Saturday night.

"But Chopper..."

"I said get out of here!" Chopper growled.

It may well have gone smoother for the Hardwood's and Agnes if it wasn't for Ike Rayburn.

The huge burly man stood up and kicked his chair out of the way and unveiled a large Bowie knife that he kept sheathed on his belt.

"Hey asshole, they're playing our song." He grinned a crooked grin, his toothpick quivering between his gritted teeth as he held the knife out in front of him, "Wanna dance?"

Beau Tooth turned to face him and seemed surprised at the big man's spunk.

"Ike, I don't think you should..."

"Quit your yapping, Hank! Somebody's got to teach this outsider some manners."

He strode towards Beau Tooth who gripped the axe handle tighter with anticipation. The knife swipe was quick and slick and the blade wedged in Tooth's gut through the thick layer of human flesh he wore underneath his decomposing plaid shirt.

"What do you think about that, big man?" Ike scoffed only to realise that the knife was wedged in place and would not give.

Tooth smiled at Ike, he could see that there was fear in the big man's eyes. Instinctively Ike lashed out and hit the mighty brute in the face with a right hand that rocked him, but had little lasting effects. Ike struck him several times in the face and torso, but Tooth stood anchored to the floorboards, taking each attack as though he was enjoying it. Perhaps he was taking such punishment to feel something he hadn't felt in many years, or perhaps he was just toying with Ike Rayburn.

"Had enough?" Ike said, backing away, his breaths now heavy and laboured, his hands rested on his thighs as he leaned over on the verge of being sick, the toothpick hung from his bottom lip held on by nothing but spittle.

Ike didn't see the axe head until it was too late, in fact the whole bar seemed to see the attack in slow motion, each person unable to do anything about it as it came hurtling down towards Ike's head and burying itself in the top of his skull.

There was a moment of shocked silence as Beau Tooth retrieved the axe from Ike's skull and there was a sickening groan from him as the toothpick fell from his mouth and a waterfall of blood and bile poured forth as he collapsed onto the floor, dead.

The screams came in unison and Agnes and Wendy scrambled to get behind the bar as Chopper shielded them holding his baseball bat tightly.

"You bastard!" Cried Hank who was the first to respond as he leapt from his chair and unloaded his revolver at the menacing brute that was still standing over Ike's body surveying his handiwork.

"You mother! Die!" Hank cried like a harpy as his revolver led the way, six bullets whistling through the air, two hit a dart board, double top and outer bull (a score of 65). A stray bullet sunk into a stag's head hanging on the wall and the remaining three hit the target. One clipped Tooth's left shoulder, one drove into his thick huge thigh and the final one connected with his bicep, causing him to drop the axe. The bullet stopped suddenly, lodging itself in place as a trickle of blood worked its way through his torn plaid shirt.

The final bullet seemed to get his attention and Hank grinned with expectancy, but Tooth snarled like a wild animal and reached out with his right hand at the oncoming gunman, a gunman that had gotten too close and now realised that he was out of bullets. His huge hand covered Hank's face and took him by surprise, he couldn't breathe from being smothered and dropped the gun as he clawed at the brute's hand, scratching away at his already heavily scarred flesh that was blackened with frostbite and stained with a layer of crusted blood. Tooth pulled him in closer, seizing his head with his other hand and squeezed viciously like a vice. Hank screamed as his eyeballs bulged and blood vessels started to break, sending forth a trickle of bloodied tears. Beau was merciful at least and ended it quickly with a quick jerk of his wrists, snapping Hank's neck and releasing him to join his friend on the floor. Tooth gazed around as if gesturing who was next to try him.

"Get the hell out of here, Wendy!" Chopper shouted, "Through the cellar! NOW!"

"But we can't leave you?" Agnes cried.

"It'll be okay, dear. Come on, let's move!" Wendy said and gestured to the trapdoor behind the bar that led to the cellar. She yanked at the handle but she didn't have the strength to move it.

"It won't budge!" Wendy screamed as she frantically tugged on the handle.

"Christ!" Chopper growled and clambered behind the bar to see if he could help.

The girl of the young couple made a run for the door but Tooth reached out and grabbed her by her hair causing her to shriek wildly. Her partner stepped in chivalrously to stop him, but got a hand around his throat for his trouble and Tooth lifted him up from the floor and the man started to cry and wet his pants, a dark patch immediately appearing on the crotch area of his jeans. Tooth discarded him and then went back to the struggling girl that was only hanging on by the combined strength of her follicles. The young man sat in a puddle of his own urine, holding his throat with terror in his eyes and the taste of salted tears on his lips. He gasped as he watched helplessly as his beloved was hoisted into the air by her hair and slammed down through the table. The young man shrieked as the table exploded in a mass of splinters and ice cream smothered him as the poor girl was hoisted up again and slammed through another table.

"P-Please stop, y-you're k-killing her!" He spluttered.

Tooth let go of her, leaving her to fall broken through another table, dead, her limbs still twitching violently. The young man threw up as Beau Tooth stalked him, but he was halted in his tracks as a wooden chair slammed into his back and exploded. Tooth grimaced and turned to see the Berquist brothers glaring back at him, young Ben had his knife drawn and Ira lifted up a bottle by its neck, beer seeped from it frantically as if it was in a hurry to leave its glass confines. He smashed the base of it against the table, leaving it with a threatening maw of jagged glass.

"That's enough, Tooth!" Ira growled, as the beast looked at him confused by the use of a name that had once meant everything to him, now it was nothing but a shadow in the back of his deranged mind.

"Yeah, I know who you are!" Ira nodded, "And the truck stops here."

Ira swiped the bottle at Tooth's face and the glass tore away flesh from his cheek and a clump of brittle hair from his beard. Tooth growled and swiped a hand at him but Ira ducked and then his young brother Ben drove his knife into his side.

"Take that you piece of shit!" Ben spluttered with tears in his eyes, stabbing him over and over again until the blade got wedged again between Tooth's flesh and the suit of others that he wore beneath.

Tooth head butted Ben, sending him falling backwards over a table as Tooth surveyed that there were now two protruding knives in his torso. Ira took another swipe with the broken bottle but met only the cotton of his shirt and then he was too close for comfort and Tooth unsheathed both blades from himself and drove one into Ira's stomach holding him in position. Ira gasped as the blade met his innards and his body fell limp

214

before the second blade appeared and slid into his throat and severed his oesophagus, leaving blood to weep from his wounds as he died quickly.

"NO!" Ben wailed as he tackled Tooth, hitting him with such force that he dropped the knives and was forced back against the wall. The tearful Ben roared as he unleashed a frenzy of fists into Tooth's face and torso.

Drunken Donald watched on in a haze, the whiskey glass still hovering at his lips.

The young man who sat in his own filth, finally woke up from the nightmare of his lover jittering uncontrollably on a broken table. He peeled himself out of his own piss and made a run for it out of the bar.

"Fucking door!" Chopper growled as he put all his might into opening it, but it wouldn't seem to budge.

"I told you it needed fixing months ago!" Wendy moaned.

"Now is not the time, woman!" Chopper snapped.

"Here, try this!" Agnes said, handing him a crowbar from a toolbox that sat underneath the bar.

Chopper slid the crowbar in-between the narrow gap of the door and Wendy and Agnes grabbed the handle and heaved as Chopper put all his bodyweight against the crowbar to lever it.

"Altogether now!" He groaned and with as much force as they could muster they managed the task and the cellar door burst open.

"Now get the hell down there!" Chopper insisted, ushering them down the old wooden steps into the darkness of the cellar.

"Chopper I..." Wendy tried to speak, grasping his hand in hers as she disappeared into the cellar.

"Just go, Wendy. I love you." Chopper smiled and kissed her hand, there were tears in her eyes as he closed the door on them.

In the darkness of the cellar Agnes shivered.

"What do we do now?" Agnes asked.

"There is a door leading onto the street, it's where the kegs are delivered. Come on, let's get out of here."

Even in the darkness Agnes knew Wendy was crying and she reached out and held her hand as they blindly made their way to the exit.

Tooth had had enough and struck Ben Berquist so hard in the face that it rocked him on his heels but before he could collapse Tooth seized him by the scruff of his neck and drove him headfirst through the jukebox which put a sudden end to *Monty Python's* humorous ditty about Tooth's former profession. The glass shattered on impact, the broken shards and smashed vinyls lacerated Ben's face and throat and he slid lifeless from the machine that sparked suddenly and died in a plume of smoke.

"BEAU!" Cried Chopper as he slammed the baseball bat into the back of his head, actually sending the behemoth down to one knee. Tooth knelt, shaking away the effects of the blow as Chopper stood over him and slammed the bat down again and again repeatedly over his head, shoulders and back.

Beau Tooth remained on a knee, trying to shake off the effects of Chopper's baseball bat. Chopper backed away to lean on a booth to catch his breath, he was no spring chicken and was no longer used to such strenuous activities.

"I can't believe it's come to this." Chopper panted, shaking his head in despair, his face was gaunt all of a sudden, showing his age.

Beau Tooth started to rise and his tendons were taut with anger, tugging at his muscles as he growled with annoyance.

"Beau?" Chopper said, his tone was melancholy, almost a whisper.

Tooth halted with his back to Chopper and for a moment his whole body seemed to relax.

"Beau? Look at me damn you!" Chopper snivelled, seething with emotion.

Tooth stood upright and looked back over his shoulder, there were wounds that ruptured blood, it was thick and dark and dribbling from stab wounds and bullet holes, but he still gave no signs that these wounds troubled him. Chopper looked into the blurred eyeball and it no longer resembled the eyes of the man he knew all those years ago.

"Why Beau? That's the one question that I ask of you? Why all the death? Why all the destruction?"

Beau turned away from Chopper with only an animalistic grunt as a reply.

"Do you even have an answer?"

Tooth ignored him and trudged back towards his axe and lifted it from the ground, its head still dripping with the blood and grey matter of Ike Rayburn.

"Beau!" He growled and Tooth spun to face him, eyes burning and hostile.

"It's not you anymore, is it?" Chopper said with a shake of his head as he clutched the baseball bat and backed away from the stalking Tooth, who gripped the axe tightly and turned the splintered shaft in his fingers, unaffected by the shards of wood that dug into his scarred flesh.

"What happened to the man I knew?" Chopper shook his head as he continued to back away towards

218

the gigantic hunting prize of Bigelow the Bear.

"My friend has truly gone. There's nothing left of him, is there?"

Chopper's back met the belly of the bear and it halted him, backed into a corner Beau Tooth seemed to like it that way, which appeared to show in his movements as he approached.

"You're nothing but a wolf in sheep's clothing!" Chopper growled and lashed out with his bat but Tooth grabbed it with his free hand and tore it away from his grip.

"Damn you, Beau. Damn you to hell for what you did to those kids of yours." Chopper grizzled as tears trickled down his face.

Tooth launched the bat across the bar and approached Chopper who could now smell the foul stench of Tooth's breath, the rancidity of it caused him to gag. Chopper grasped the thick fur of the taxidermy grizzly bear behind him that towered over him and Tooth, his fingertips ran across the harshness of the fraying length of rope that held the creature in place.

Chopper smiled and Tooth halted just inches away from the cornered landlord and tilted his head like some animal that couldn't comprehend why his prey was wearing a look of smugness.

"Good old, Bigelow." Chopper said and tugged on the rope as hard as he could, before throwing himself onto the floor and out of the way of the gigantic Bigelow as he fell forward and landed on top of Beau Tooth, grounding him. Tooth growled and grimaced as he tussled from side to side trying to free himself from the massive weight of the bear that smothered him.

Chopper got to his feet and quickly headed for the exit, but his eyes glanced around his establishment and gazed with remorse at those that had fallen.

Ben Berquist lay in a heap on the floor, his face and throat lacerated by glass and broken pieces of vinyl. The young woman, her spine and neck twisted into an irregular shape.

Ira Berquist's stomach and throat still leaking plasma all over the wooden floorboards, seeping through the cracks.

Hank Jessop with his head turned all the way around staring at him with his dead eyes and Ira Rayburn's massive bulk face down on the floor with a wedge cut out of his skull.

Chopper turned around and around gazing at the deer, raccoon and cougar heads mounted on the wooden slatted walls, their eyes judging him for fleeing when he had the chance to finish this.

He turned to look back at Tooth who was still struggling to free himself from the bulk of the mighty Bigelow.

"I can end this." He whispered, "God help me, that's what I'm going to do!"

Chopper marched over towards him and lifted up Tooth's axe and hoisted it up above his head, Tooth stared into his eyes, perhaps into his soul and he grinned. Chopper believed that the true Beau Tooth was hidden inside somewhere and this is what he wanted, he wanted it to end.

"Sorry, old friend." Chopper said and he brought the axe hurtling down towards Tooth who rolled to the side and the axe head bit nothing but the back of Bigelow the bear, tearing through the fur and dried flesh releasing a cloud of sawdust from within into the air, momentarily blinding him.

Chopper dropped the axe and held his eyes as the dust attacked his face and he called out in discomfort. As he wiped away the excess and the cloud dispersed he noticed that the broken Bigelow lay alone on the floor.

"Shit." Chopper whined and turned to face Beau Tooth who seized him by the throat and hoisted him into the air, marching him over to the wall and driving him through a large pair of stag's antlers that was mounted on the wall. Chopper gasped as the antlers broke through his rib cage and then his fleshy torso before erupting with blood. He coughed and spluttered, blood dribbling from his mouth as Beau Tooth stood admiring his work that hung on the wall like a piece of art in a gallery. Chopper hung on the antlers, his feet shaking for a moment before going limp and as his eyes began to close he heard Beau Tooth speak in a ghostly gravelly tone that trembled in the back of his throat.

"*Friend.*"

Chopper died going to hell with that terrifying voice trembling in his ears as he passed through to the other side, he hung there lifeless on the antlers and the bar was silent.

Tooth turned and strode towards the exit grabbing the carcass of Ira Berquist and throwing him over his shoulder while seizing the broken twisted carcass of the young Woman by her hair and dragged her along the floor as he left the bar, axe still gripped in his mitt as if his life depended on it.

Drunken Donald had not moved a muscle during the whole ordeal and he stared in horror as the beast left the bar, the whiskey glass still hovering by his trembling bottom lip. He blinked several times, not knowing whether what he had witnessed was reality or the work of the seven glasses of Moondog Whiskey he'd put away that evening. He slowly lowered the glass onto the table and pushed it away.

CHAPTER 25

The cellar hatch at the rear of *Chopper's Bar* was cumbersome to open, a foot of snow had gathered upon it making it very difficult for Wendy and Agnes to manoeuvre. Finally after a considerable amount of effort they were able to force the door open and exit from the stifling closeness of the cellar and breathe-in the cold night air.

"I thought we were never going to get out of there." Agnes said as she climbed out into the alleyway that was sandwiched in-between the bar and Sullivan's convenience store.

Wendy remained silent as she struggled to lift herself out from the cellar. Agnes could see that she was upset, her lined face looked pale and her mascara had run down her cheeks giving her a haunting illusion of black tears.

"Let me help you." Agnes said and held Wendy's hand and hauled her up into the snow clad alley.

"Thank you." Came Wendy's reply, but she couldn't bring herself to meet Agnes's gaze.

Agnes didn't know what to say, she was elated that they had managed to escape the massacre that was taking place inside, but she could not imagine how Wendy felt about leaving her husband to whatever fate Beau Tooth wished to dish out.

"Are you okay?" She asked, feeling foolish for even asking the question for she already knew the answer.

"Of course I'm not!" Wendy snapped and pulled herself away from Agnes's grip and bounded halfway down the alleyway before coming to a sliding halt in the snow and then turning back and walking half way back. She wrapped arms around herself, suddenly feeling the chill and it was obvious from the aching look on her face that fear had taken hold of her.

Agnes ran to join her and embraced her.

"It's gonna be okay, we can get away from here. We'll be okay. I promise!"

Wendy nodded, but looked as though her mind was faraway, other thoughts danced before her mind's eye, thoughts of death, a nightmare vision of a life without her husband and it seemed to be all too much for her that she broke down and began to cry.

"It's okay, it's okay." Agnes said, stroking her hair away from her moist face, strands sticking to her flesh like plump worms.

"But it won't be!" Wendy cried and once again pushed her away, "How can I leave my husband? How can I walk away from my Bruce?"

"He gave us time so that we could get away. That's what he wanted for you. To get away from here and be safe."

"I can't leave him! I won't leave him!" Wendy cried and ran down the alleyway towards the high street. Her loafers were unfit for the conditions and caused her to slip several times before losing her footing and tumbling to the ground. She picked herself up and still managed to carry on.

Agnes could almost hear the woman's heart breaking as she ran, her loafers breaking through the hard crust of snow that lay untouched.

"Wendy!" She called after her, but it was no use, there was no way she was going to stop her with words with her being in such a state of emotional anguish.

Wendy struggled through the snow, slipping and sliding as she was about to reach the high street. Her aim was obviously to turn the corner and go back into the bar, but Agnes grabbed her from behind and pulled her in close, falling against the unforgiving brick wall of the bar.

"What the hell are you doing?" Wendy growled as she tried to free herself, "Let go of me!"

Agnes silenced her by wrapping a cold hand over her mouth and held her tightly as she wriggled frantically to prise herself free.

"Stop this." Agnes hissed in a whisper, "He's out there!"

Wendy's eyes moved over to the high street where the sledge stood, the rear of it piled with bodies, sure enough there was Beau Tooth adding the carcasses of the young woman and Ira Berquist to his ever growing harvest of death.

"The reaper has come." Agnes said, her voice a ghostly quiver of nothingness that rode on a plume of ice cold air.

She slid her hand slowly away from Wendy's mouth, as she did a gasp escaped from the warmth of Wendy's quivering maw.

"I-I can't leave him." Wendy whispered.

"If you want to stay alive, you must!"

Beau Tooth propped his axe up against the sledge and trudged back towards the bar, the door hung crookedly on its hinges and the brute just about fit through the entrance as he disappeared inside.

Agnes released Wendy and peered around the corner, watching on as he disappeared inside once again.

"This is our chance Wendy, we have to get out of here."

"But..." Wendy grizzled, traumatised by the whole ordeal with images of Beau Tooth carrying Chopper from the bar and being slapped on top of the others like a piece of meat.

"Listen!" Agnes growled at her while grabbing her arms and shaking her.

"You're hurting me! Let go!" Wendy snivelled.

"Listen to me, you have to let it go or we are as good as dead ourselves."

"How the hell can I let it go?" Wendy said, her feisty old persona rearing its head again as she pushed Agnes away from her, scowling defiantly.

"You must!"

"Easy for you to say, that's my husband in there. I can't bear it. I can't."

"You will have to learn to or else you will meet the same fate. Do you think that's what Chopper would have wanted?"

"What do you know about anything? What do you know about loss?" Wendy growled before immediately glowing with embarrassment, "Your brother... I'm sorry."

Agnes's head dropped and she gazed at anything but Wendy's eyes of pity.

"I have had to come to terms with it that my brother is dead." Agnes said, "And if we continue with this merry-go-round then we will be too."

227

Wendy dropped her head in shame and grief and nodded in agreement.

"Okay, then we have to make a run for it. Do you think you can run?" Agnes asked.

"I think so." Wendy said with a nod of her head, wiping away the tears that stained her face with mascara.

"Where's the best place to go? Think now, the safest place away from this bastard."

"It has to be the Sheriff's office."

"Shit!" Agnes gasped, "Sheriff Russell!" She realised that with everything that had happened, she had completely forgotten about the Sheriff.

"He's probably dead too." Wendy sighed.

"No, he can't be..." Agnes replied, but knew that Wendy was probably right. If he was alive why wasn't he here when the town needed him the most.

"Right, so we head for the Sheriff's office." Agnes said matter-of-factly and the pair attempted to step out onto the street but were halted at the sight of Beau Tooth exiting again with the bulk of Ira Rayburn draped over his shoulders as though he were a prize stag that he had just been put out of its misery. In his hands he dragged Ben Berquist and Hank Jessop by their feet through the snow. A trail of blood seeped out behind them staining the luscious snow all manner of pink tones.

As he continued to load up, Agnes grabbed hold of Wendy.

"We need to go now, while he's distracted."

"B-But he'll surely see us!" Wendy gasped.

"He is far too busy with those bodies to notice us."

"Oh God!" She whined, but she agreed and the pair crept out from around the alleyway as Tooth's back was turned and they crept quietly across the sidewalk that luckily for them had been shuffled earlier by Old Sparky so there was no breaking of fresh snow to give away their position.

The pair tried not to look at the ghostly faces of the dead that gawped at them as if calling for help.

Agnes moved with swiftness along the sidewalk past the entrance of the bar and then the row of various shops, all of them closed up for the night. She spotted that there was another alley between Wellington's pharmacy and a florists and smiled as she knew they could disappear into it and be safely out of sight. As she turned to inform Wendy of her plan she skidded to a halt.

"No, Wendy, don't." She said to herself as Wendy stood frozen, staring into the bar observing her loving husband mounted on the wall like some hunting prize. She shook her head relentlessly and started cursing the very name of God and with an agonising scream that turned Agnes's blood cold she collapsed to her knees in an uncontrollable puddle.

The sound got Tooth's attention and he spun around on the spot, his eyes growing wide with malice and anticipation, he allowed Ira's bulk to fall from his back and into the snow with a thud as though he were some heavyweight boxer disrobing and readying himself for the bout. Kicking up blood stained snow with each stride, he bounded over towards Wendy, who was knelt and sobbing loudly.

Agnes heard herself call to stop the beast but there was no stopping a great white shark when it had the scent of blood quivering around his nostrils. He grabbed her from behind, both hands clamped to each side of her head and he hoisted her into the air. Her screams were bloodcurdling and immediately several lights from apartments above the shops burst into life and illuminated the street, curtains twitched and lights went off. No one wanted to deal with what was going on out on the street.

"Bastards!" Agnes growled, looking up at one window and making eye contact with a man who seemed to sigh before drawing the curtain back and turning off his light, "You could help! You could do something!" She growled and scooped up a snowball and launched it at the window, but neither the curtains opened nor the light came back on.

As Agnes turned back to witness Tooth remove the head from Wendy's body with a final yank she fell silent as her body fell lifeless to the ground. Blood leaked out from Wendy's neck and melted the snow with its heat, steam rising up around Tooth as he stood exploring the head in his hands, the spinal cord still attached to it dangling freely as it dripped blood into the snow. He separated the skull from the spinal-cord with one vicious tug and dropped the head in the snow, rejecting it, while he retrieved the body and dragged it across the street to join the others.

"Run you fool, run!" Agnes growled to herself, her teeth gritted so hard she was sure that they would crack at any moment. She couldn't leave it and something spurred her back up towards the street and towards the chaos.

"What the hell am I doing?" She asked herself and then called Tooth's name as she marched towards him. His eyes glistened again in the shard of a streetlamp and picked up his axe and bounded down the middle of the road to meet her.

CHAPTER 26

Agnes knelt down in the middle of the road, the knees of her jeans becoming sodden with the cold, damp snow. She slipped off her rucksack and placed it down in front of her, her fingers shook wildly with angst as she struggled with the zipper.

"Shit! Shit! Shit! Blasted thing!" She grumbled all the while paying close attention to Beau Tooth as he trudged through the snow towards her.

Tooth's pace slowed as he contemplated what the girl in front of him was up to. She intrigued him so much that he felt like he needed to take his time with this particular prey. He wanted to understand her before he killed her.

She suddenly let out a yelp and retracted her hand quickly as if she had been bitten.

The palm of her right hand was cut and bleeding, a shard of her broken laptop screen protruding out of the wound. She squealed as she pulled it out and discarded it and the blood dripped into the snow as she hissed through the pain. She sunk her hand into the snow hoping it would numb the pain, the ice cold bitterness denied her wishes.

Tooth stopped and smiled, he licked his lips before carrying on towards her, wounded prey was the best sort of prey.

"Sicko!" She growled and delved into her rucksack once more, removing the broken laptop and discarding it.

"Where is it! Where is it!" She grumbled as she searched.

Tooth trudged ever closer.

"Got it!" Agnes cried and pulled out the flare gun, aiming it at the great hulking behemoth that stalked her.

At the sight of the barrel pointed at him he came to a halt and pondered again, the girl was an enigma to him, he had never encountered anyone like her before and a part of him felt a little apprehensive. He truly believed that she would indeed pull the trigger and send a flare hurtling towards him.

"This is for my brother you sick fuck!" She growled, rising up from the snow and pulling the trigger.

Nothing happened. Again and again her clammy hands struggled to activate the gun and the blood seeping from her palm caused the handle to slip and it slid in her grip.

"Shit!" She whined.

Beau Tooth seemed more disappointed than anything that he almost sighed. Did he want a flare gun to penetrate his chest and end his sordid life? Who could say for sure, but he moved forward with a quicker pace, perhaps believing that this girl wasn't something different after all. Just prey like all the others.

By the time she had figured out that the locking lever was still in place and that was obstructing her from activating the flare it was too late and Tooth was on her. He swept a hand across her face sending her tumbling to the ground, her glasses falling from her face and becoming lost in the snow as the flare gun left her hands and fell near her open rucksack, which thankfully did not explode.

Agnes pulled herself out of the snow, her cheek was burning from the swipe, her head was spinning uncontrollably, she couldn't focus, but she instinctively looked for her glasses, sieving through the snow.

Tooth towered over her casting a menacing shadow as she finally found her glasses, as she placed them back on, the left lens had a small hairline fracture across it that gave the illusion that her eyeball had been sliced in half.

Tooth grabbed a handful of her hair and lifted her out of the snow and off the ground, she screamed and kicked her legs frantically, anything she could do to hamper his grip on her hair, he slammed her down on the road. Even the thick layer of snow did little to cushion the impact and she felt ribs crack as she came down on her side. She groaned and struggled for breath, her whole innards had been shaken by the violent jolt and she lay gasping.

Beau Tooth flicked away the thick strands of her hair that he still had wrapped around his fingers and closed in again lifting her up by the hood of her parka. She was too delirious to put up much of a fight this time, all the energy seemed to have been knocked out of her and she hung there from the hood gasping.

The Volkswagen Beetle that belonged to Gertrude Cassidy still burned on and Tooth walked over towards the flames that rose from the car.

Agnes realised what he was planning and instantly started to struggle again, adrenaline had kicked in now and she had a second wind allowing her to fight on.

He held her close to the fire, she could feel the heat stifling her, the flames licking at her like the tongues of hungry wolves. He held her closer still as flames lapped at her feet, her toes inside wriggling from the excessive heat that threatened to burn them.

Thinking fast she unzipped the parka and fell out of it onto the snow, the parka suddenly became very light and Tooth realised she had slipped out of it and she was scrambling along the road towards her rucksack and the flare gun.

Tooth growled and threw the parka onto the flames where the fire ate it up quickly, the material causing the flames to turn green and spit out the feathers within that were consumed easily.

Agnes crawled towards the flare gun and grabbed its handle but Tooth's foot crunched down on her injured hand and forced her to release it.

He grabbed her by her throat and began to lift her up but she remained defiant and fought against his advances scratching at his face and eyes with her fingernails, opening new scars and old. He halted her advances quickly with a violent squeeze of her windpipe and she seemingly gave up the fight, her face turning a peculiar bluish colour. As he lifted her up he did not realise that she had grasped the broken laptop and she slammed it into his forehead, it smashed completely over his head causing him to drop her.

She hit the floor and she watched on gasping for that cold night air as he pulled shards of glass, plastic and circuit board out of his face.

He had had enough of games now and hoisted the axe above his head as the wailing of a car horn suddenly echoed up the high street and a Sheriff Office issue Ford F150 Lariat came sliding across the snow hurtling towards them. Tooth turned to face the out of control vehicle as Agnes crawled out of harms way just as the vehicle slammed into Tooth and forced him violently through the window of the old abandoned hardware shop that had once belonged to Old Sparky. Tooth disappeared inside and so did the front of the vehicle as Agnes watched on in dismay.

The blue and red lights suddenly came on and lit up the area and there was a whooping holler from the siren but it died quickly as if the lights and siren had been activated as an afterthought by the driver.

The front of the store was completely demolished and steam had started to hiss out of the hood of the vehicle and it squealed like a boiling kettle.

Agnes grabbed her rucksack and dropped the flare gun back inside absently as she slipped her arms back through the loops, all the while she watched on. Watching the vehicle, hoping that the driver was okay, watching the broken storefront hoping that Tooth was not.

"Are you okay?" She called out, over the last few moments lights had illuminated the high street once again as those above in apartments found that there was just way too much going on for them to ignore it any longer. They stood at their windows glaring down at the police vehicle submerged in the glass and rubble of the store.

Still there was no movement from within and that filled Agnes with relief and she shuffled forwards slowly towards the vehicle to check on the driver.

She gazed in through the window and saw the body of a man slumped over the steering wheel. She banged at the window and the body stirred, she could hear his groans from outside.

She opened the door and Deputy Raymond Clegg sat back in his seat holding his head in his hands.

"Deputy! Are you okay?" Agnes asked.

He groaned again and blinked his eyes to focus on her, a fine line of blood trickled down from his hairline and down his long slender nose.

"Please don't be alarmed Miss, help is on the way." He stuttered, slurring every other word, it sounded routine and mechanical as though this was what he said on such occasions.

"You're delirious." She said undoing his seatbelt and sliding him out of the front seat.

"What are you doing to me?" He grumbled trying to fight her off.

"Don't struggle." She growled, dragging him away from the car.

"Where are you taking me? Let go of me." He struggled so much he fell into the snow and she grabbed the collar of his parka and pulled him through the snow away from the scene as far as she could.

"I've got to get you away from there. I don't like the look of that hood."

Smoke was bellowing out from the twisted metal as though it were the snorting of some mechanical dragon.

"You have the right to remain... remain... remain..." Clegg slurred.

"Silent." Agnes finished the sentence helping him up into a seated position.

"That's the one!" Clegg laughed, "Oh, my head is banging."

"You're going to be alright now." She said and picked up a ball of snow and slipped it down the back of his neck.

Deputy Clegg squealed and jumped up onto his feet, his body gyrating as the ice and snow tricked down his back, but it was enough to bring him round.

"What the devil is going on?" He cried.

"I think you killed Beau Tooth." She said pointing towards the crash, both of them turned to face the carnage.

"Really?" Clegg said with astonishment causing his face to blush, "I did that?"

"Yep." Agnes smiled and clapped him on the back, "Hell of a job, Deputy."

For a second he felt proud and his chest seemed to expand and he tipped his head back so his nose was in the air.

"Yes, it was, wasn't it." He said arrogantly.

"Okay, well don't pose for your statue just yet, because I think that engine is gonna..."

And blow it did, sending the pair diving away from the blast as the car's engine erupted in a raging inferno.

They lay in the snow looking up at the fire as it took the inside of the hardware store too, there were more explosions from inside where old cans of paint that had been left there when it closed erupted too. Each explosion sent a new wave of glass and rubble out into the air and it fell onto them as if it were competing with the snow to see what could hit the ground first.

"Oh shit, that's coming out of my wages." Clegg sighed as he got to his feet and put his hands on his hips as he took in the scene.

Agnes was left to fend for herself and pulled her own bruised and battered carcass out of a pile of snow.

The store was spitting fire angrily and the vehicle constantly weeped gas that was immediately lapped up by the flames. The siren squealed again for a short while before it died completely as if it were a sow being led to slaughter.

"So what happened here, Miss?" Clegg said as he turned to face her, his face was stern and his hand remained on his hips, he spoke to her as if all of this was her fault.

But before Agnes could answer an axe came swirling through the flames and lodged itself into Deputy Clegg's spine. He lurched forwards almost toppling on top of her, he murmured words that were incoherent and then coughed out a wad of blood into his hands. His eyes were sad as he looked at her for help and then collapsed face down into the snow, the axe rising out of his back.

"No!" She whimpered, shaking her head with disbelief as she backed away from the fallen Deputy and her gaze shifted to the burning store as the hulking shape of Beau Tooth emerged through the flames.

He stepped out onto the street once again, his torn clothes flickering with tiny flames as they burned feverishly. Tooth did not seem to notice but marched towards her to retrieve his axe and perhaps his final victim.

She slid back into the snow and searched for Clegg's sidearm. She retrieved it and slid off the safety and managed to pull the trigger, but the force of it sent her off balance and she tumbled backwards into the snow. The bullet hit nothing but the rear tail light of the burning 4x4 as Tooth retrieved the axe, yanking it tightly. Clegg's lifeless corpse rose with it and Tooth had to shake his axe free, finally the body fell back into the snow, fresh viscera dripping from the axe's head.

She knelt on the floor and aimed the gun at him again, but he was within reach of her now and he swept the gun out of her hands with a thrust of the axe. She felt several of her fingers break and she held them closely to her bosom as she cried out. Tears came again and she looked up to him with helpless moist eyes like that of a doe, she was ready for it to end. The bite of the axe slid gently up to her throbbing temples as if to line up the perfect swipe that would take her scalp off, she closed her eyes and waited for the inevitable.

"Do it." She whispered, "I've had enough."

The axe head was cold against her head, but she found that she craved it, she was spent.

He brought the axe away and readied himself until something halted him and he squinted out into the distance. The distant sound of what sounded like hornets stopped him in his tracks.

The two Bobcat snowmobiles hurtled up the high street towards the beacon of flames that lit their destination. Astride the vehicles were Officer's Ouellet and Huffman with determination leading the way through the flurry of snow from the sky and the wave that kicked up at them from the skis that cut through its icy crispness.

Beau Tooth left Agnes kneeling with her eyes clenched shut and expecting death and stepped out into the middle of the road, he swivelled the axe around and dropped the head of it into the snow as he held it at his side to welcome the new arrivals.

"There he is!" Called Huffman.

"Fuck me he is real after all!" Ouellet replied in a thick French accent.

"Look at the size of that mother!" Huffman added.

"The bigger they are." Ouellet said and accelerated ahead of his colleague leaving snow to blind Huffman's way and slow him down considerably.

Officer Ouellet drove towards Tooth as if the pair were playing a game of chicken, neither looked as though they were about to give way until at the last spilt second Officer Ouellet's snowmobile swept past the unmoving Tooth and slid off course where he span to a halt and had to rev up the Bobcat again.

The flurry of snow caused by Ouellet's spin drifted in front of the oncoming Huffman who could no longer see and when the flurry had cleared all he saw was the head of a bloodied axe grind to an immediate halt in his face, sweeping him from the snowmobile which continued on without him and came to sudden halt through a book shop window.

Agnes watched on as Officer Huffman fell at the feet of Beau Tooth and the brute turned on the spot to meet Officer Ouellet who came again on the Bobcat, determination etched on his face that he would not be swerving away this time, he meant to go straight through the murdering bastard once and for all.

Tooth fought dirty and swept his axe across the layer of snow at his feet and it blinded Ouellet's path causing him to loose control and hurtle straight into the back of the Volkswagen Beetle, exploding into a ball of flame on impact that engulfed him and burned him to a black cinder where he sat.

Agnes scrambled away to cower in a doorway of a shop, she saw that he was scouring the street for her but when she could not be seen he hoisted up Deputy Clegg and Officer Huffman's dead carcasses and carried them over to his sledge. Ouellet was left to burn, his blacked crisp flesh and bones of char were of no use to Tooth.

He stood surveying the scene, the chaos that had been left behind from his little visit to the town.

There was a shuffling sound and it caught his attention as the ghostly figure of Marlena Pascoe came waddling past him. She wore nothing but her nightgown and her feet were again bare, but the cold did not seem to bother her as her mind was lost somewhere in the past.

"Hello there Beau." She said.

Tooth looked at her with a strange curiosity and whenever anyone mentioned his name it seemed to scratch away at the back of his skull as though he should know what it meant.

"It's been a while since I last saw you. Strapping young fellow, yes sir! I always told my Elroy you were likely to break some hearts in Maple Falls."

Marlena Pascoe smiled, her eyes were miles away though as if looking somewhere else, another time and place, a happier time and place.

Beau Tooth gripped the handle of his axe and lifted it up to be cradled in his meaty hands, but he just stared at her, the animal instinct that spurred him on had seemed to subside for the moment and all he could do was watch her.

"Have you seen Elroy by the way? He's ever so late for his sup." She said and then turned away from him and shuffled down the street, "Nice seeing you Beau, give my love to Marcy and the girls."

Agnes watched from her hiding place with a hand over her mouth, unbelieving of what she had just witnessed, Tooth watched Marlena walk away as she continued to ask herself where her husband was.

He turned away from her and his attention back to the sledge where he slid the axe into a crevice at the front of it, where there would have once been a seat a long time ago when it was drawn by horses, but that had been a lifetime ago, now it was nothing more than a shelf which held several other tools within. He gazed at his prey, a mass of flailing limbs, wide eyes and drooping maws that captured the victims final moments like a polaroid and he seemed content. He looked to seize the chain and be on his way, another successful winter harvest to see him through another year.

The sound of a siren caused him to drop the chain, his hulking shoulders seemed to fall with frustration, perhaps the demon's thirst for blood and flesh had subsided and he longed to rest now.

Or maybe not.

Another Ford Lariat worked its way up the high street with Sergeant Church at the wheel, gripping it tightly and squinting through the rapid windshield wipers that pushed away the falling snow as she chewed on a fresh piece of gum.

"There's the bastard." She growled.

"I can't see shit!" Scoffed Officer Smith who rode in the passenger seat, hanging on for dear life, obviously not trusting his Sergeant's reckless driving.

"Get ready, we'll be on him any minute now."

Tooth removed something from his sledge, a long chain of rust tumbled out onto the street, unwinding to unveil its full length. Shards of sharp metal had been wound around every other rusted link to create a homemade spike strip and he grabbed the end of it and marched down the street before sweeping it out in front of him. He turned his back on the oncoming vehicle that bellowed at him with its high-pitched squeal and

246

flickered lights of blue and red that did little to dazzle him as he returned to the sledge, ignoring them completely.

"There he is!" Smith pointed out, a look of awe on his face.

"I see him." Snapped Sergeant Church.

"He's a... monster!" He gasped.

"Give me a break!" She scoffed, "I drive this fender up his ass and we'll see what kind of a monster he is."

She made the mistake of being over confident and reckless, the conditions as they were she should have never have been attempting such speeds, chained tyres or not. The front tyres of the Ford Lariat hit the spike strip, the rubber blew immediately on impact and the twisted metal shards coiled themselves around the chains on the tyres and sent the vehicle out of control. In Sergeant Church's defence she did an amazing job of trying to control the vehicle's crash but it flipped violently. Too much speed had built up and too much momentum had sent the car rolling over and over before it came to rest on its roof. Blues and reds dying as the officers inside sat securely upside down and unconscious.

"Jesus..." Agnes shook her head, unable to take in the carnage that her eyes had just witnessed and as she staggered out onto the street she realised that Tooth was gone.

Two dirty lines of rust and blood sliced through the snow leaving a trail back to the woods.

Agnes dropped to her knees and sobbed, her entire body hurt, bones had been splintered and broken, blood had been spilled, but still it was nothing to what it had done to her mentally.

Another Ford Lariat worked its way up the street, a sensible speed with nothing to prove, driven by Lieutenant Tammy Adams who slid out from the vehicle and ran to Agnes, she slid beside her and hugged her.

"Thank goodness, you're okay." Adams gasped holding her closely.

"I wish I could say the same for everyone else." Agnes murmured.

"What happened?"

"Beau Tooth happened."

Tammy looked around at the scene trying to take it all in and could never comprehend what had taken place.

"We have to get you out of here." Tammy said helping Agnes up, but she shook her head.

"No."

"What? What do you mean no? You are lucky to be alive. Let's be thankful for that and get you back to the office."

"He has to be stopped. We have to stop him or this will happen again and again."

Agnes marched over to her vehicle, the engine still running, the blues and reds of its light still bathing the street in its constant sequence.

Tammy Adams looked at her gobsmacked.

"Now are you gonna drive me after him or have I got to walk?" Agnes said, sliding into the passenger seat and folding her arms defiantly.

Adams finally succumbed and joined her in the vehicle. They rolled slowly and cautiously towards the woods, passing all the havoc that still littered the street in Beau Tooth's wake.

CHAPTER 27

Sheriff Russell was unable to start the Ford Lariat after painstakingly digging it out of the mountain of snow that had consumed it. He now made his way towards town on foot across the snow covered road of Maple Cross as fast as he could.

Nora raced at his side, tongue flapping in the cold breeze, her dark eyes glistening like two flecks of obsidian, as she howled with delight. To her all this felt like a game, digging and running with her new friend acted as a distraction to what she had witnessed earlier in the day. She liked her new friend.

"Don't get too excited!" The Sheriff panted trying to catch his breath, "This is not going to be a permanent relationship."

He glared at the dog who carried on her merry way oblivious to the meaning of his words.

"I'm serious!" He scoffed, "I've no room in my life for a dog. I'm struggling to look after myself as it is, without another mouth to feed."

She took his words for playfulness and bounded around him as he jogged, almost causing him to fall over in the snow.

"Watch it!" He growled, but when he looked into her dark eyes he saw his own smile reflected back at him, perhaps a companion was just what he needed. He came to a halt on the edge of the town, a blaze of flames flickering in the distance.

"Jesus!" He whispered, his eyelids flickering in disbelief.

His limbs were heavy with fatigue and stopping was the worst thing he could have done, his legs were refusing to work now, his hamstrings had gone taut and his calves were cramping. But he couldn't stop, he had to carry on, it was his job and the wellbeing of the people who lived within the town took priority over his aching joints and strained muscles.

The flames had been one thing that had caught him off guard, seeing the flickering of yellows and oranges fiercely raging up from the whiteness of the snow made it look like an enormous candle that was almost completely out of wax.

As he and Nora strode into town, the dog seemed more sheepish and hung close to him, so close that he could feel her brushing up against his knee. He instinctively knew that she felt anxious, he knew this of course as he felt exactly the same way. He offered a reassuring stroke of her head, she nuzzled his cold fingertips and licked at them, her tongue and breath was warming and that was enough of a gesture to reassure him too.

His heart sank when he saw the town and the carnage that one man had left behind in his wake, all of it concealed by a ceiling of thick black smoke.

Old Sparky's redundant hardware store burned freely, flames reaching out from a destroyed shopfront with the shell of a burnt out vehicle that resembled one of the office's Ford Lariat's spewing out from it.

Another vehicle sat smouldering, a black twisted metal cage engulfed in furious amber flame, it appeared to be a Volkswagen Beetle from its shape and style.

Two Bobcats lay neglected in the snow, one of them flickered with the last dying embers of flame. Another squad car sat over turned in the middle of the road as windows and shop fronts of various stores were completely destroyed.

But the most devastating sight that met his eyes was the amount of blood that stained the snow, it was sickening and the stench of death lingered in the air.

There was a hideous aroma of burning flesh and bone that was nauseating and maddening and it made Sheriff Russell's head spin.

For a moment he believed he may pass out, but he would not allow himself to do so.

He walked along the street taking in the scenes and made his way into *Chopper's*, he placed his hand on his side arm and flicked the strap away that held it in its holster, just in case, he had no idea what to expect.

Nora refused to step one paw inside and sat by the door, he saw her nostrils twitching.

"Death." He murmured, "She can smell the dead and she doesn't like it one bit. Can't say I blame her." He swallowed and retched, the smell was fresh and maddening to his senses.

The bar was demolished, the jukebox shattered and Chopper Hardwood's prize possession, the big bear Bigelow laid on the floor, the sawdust used in its taxidermy spilling out around it.

"I could go for a glass of Hackenschmidt right about now." He said to himself licking at his lips, they were dry with thirst and cracked from being out in the cold for so long.

Blood caked the floor which he found the hard way by slipping in it and almost going to ground, but he managed to steady himself.

"Good God, it's a massacre!" He said with a shake of his head, "All this blood and no bodies..." Those words sounded so very familiar to him, he had said that before.

He gazed around and then his eyes doubled in size and he staggered sideways before collapsing into a chair and clasping a hand over his mouth as he gazed at the latest trophy that had been added to the wall.

"No...C-Chopper..." He wheezed, his eyes became moist and it was all he could do to fight back tears as he rose slowly and then moved quickly towards his friend that was hanging from the wall. His eyes flitted and blinked rapidly at the blood that dripped from the stag's antlers that burst out through his chest. A puddle of blood had gathered underneath him that was still being added to every other second or so with a constant seeping of blood from his wounds.

"My God, Chopper, what has he done to you?" He whimpered, his eyes were no longer able to contain the tears and they fell down his chapped, red cheeks eagerly. He reached out and touched his friend's hand, it was cold, his fingers rough from years of graft and he held it as he hung there, his face gaunt and lifeless eyes shimmering in the flickering neon of the bar signs. Blood caked his moustache and bruising on his aging flesh made him look almost unrecognisable.

"What the hell happened?" He asked and was immediately taken aback when he got a response.

"He got fucked up." A mumble came from the corner of the bar.

Sheriff Russell turned quickly, sliding in blood and smearing it into the floorboards. His gun slid out of the holster with instinct taking over, aiming his handgun at the figure that sat in the booth.

"He fucked them all up." The voice said again.

"Donald is that you?" The Sheriff asked and he slid his sidearm back into its holster and quickly made his way over to the booth.

"Yeah, it's me, Sheriff. Well, at least I think it's me. Hard to tell to be honest with ya, after witnessing what I've just seen."

Donald Bass's face was as pale as the snow that fell from the sky outside and he sat upright and alert with scared eyes wide and creased with veins as though he had been hypnotised.

The Sheriff made an unfair judgement and his eyes initially focused on the glass that sat in front of him. But on closer inspection he could see that it had hardly been touched. He knew Donald well and knew that a glass didn't stay full long if it sat in front of 'Drunken Old Bass'.

"I haven't touched it, Sheriff." He said, following his gaze, "I'm as sober as I've ever been right now. In fact I may never drink again."

"What happened here, Donald? Can you remember?"

"Remember?!" He chuckled, almost hysterical was the sound and he shook his head slowly, "I'll never fucking forget it I know that much. At first I thought it was the booze, I mean I'd been hitting it pretty hard you know, well it is Friday."

This meant nothing Sheriff Russell knew, Bass hit it hard with any day of the week that had a Y in it.

Sheriff found himself judging the man and immediately regretted it believing that he himself was following exactly the same path as Donald Bass. If he continued on his own slippery slope of chasing lady liquor then he would be sitting in the same position a few years from now.

"Tell me what happened, Donald." Russell said, sliding into the booth opposite him.

"He just burst in. I've never seen anything like it, he cut through them all..."

"All? All who?"

"A young couple, looked like they were on a first date or something. Threw that girl around by her hair like a rag doll he did, and the guy, no, no. I'm wrong, he got away."

"He got away!"

"Yeah, pissed himself he did. Can't say I fucking blame him. I think my underwear is a bit moist to tell you the truth, but I have been too scared to move to check the front or the back."

"You don't know who this young couple was?"

"Not by name." He shook his head, "I've seen them around you know, I believe she works at the

256

florists. But names, no I haven't got any names. People don't seem to want to get to know you when you're the town drunk."

"I think I know the girl. Blonde, pretty..."

"That's the one." He nodded, "There was the poker players too. I mean you know that bunch they try and act like they are hard nuts. Especially that Ira Rayburn, well his nut got well and truly cracked and its shell didn't seem to be that hard to me. Split him straight down the middle of that thick ugly face of his with that great big, dirty axe."

Donald looked down at the whiskey at the thought and licked at his lips with anticipation, but seemed to change his mind and turned his attention back to The Sheriff.

"An axe." Russell whispered.

"Yep! A fucking big one!" Donald swallowed hard and reached out for the whiskey sitting in front of him, licking his lips with nervous anticipation. His hand was shaking wildly, but before he could grab the glass he clenched his fist and pulled it away.

"The others bought it too, within a blink of an eye. I mean, I know I've had a skinful, but it was like watching a movie, it happened so fast, I just couldn't believe it. I still don't."

Sheriff Russell turned back and looked at his friend Bruce Hardwood, known to all as Chopper, a friend to all.

"You don't need to worry no more about old Chopper, Sheriff."

The Sheriff turned back to face Donald.

"He gave a good showing and put up one hell of a fight."

Donald smiled and most of his teeth were rotted away, leaving yellowing nuggets rooted in red gums like gold embedded in the rock faces of some forgotten mine.

"Close to having the bastard too, he was."

"Yeah?" Sheriff Russell smiled a proud smile, it was at least good to know that he went down fighting, "Good old, Chopper."

"But close only counts in horseshoes and hand grenades. Had the chance to walk away he did, but made the mistake of coming back."

"Wendy! What about Wendy? Shit what about Agnes!" Sheriff gasped.

"If you mean that young girl with the specs, she got out through the cellar with Wendy. Should be safe enough if they made a dash for it."

"Well that's at least a relief."

"She looked shook up when she came in here though, that Agnes. Don't think she'll ever be right after this."

"Thanks Donald." The Sheriff said standing up, "You get yourself home now."

"I will try, if I can move."

Sheriff Russell gazed down at the whiskey and licked at his lips.

One for the road?

"You gonna drink that, Donald?"

"Not me. No, Sir. I'm done with the drink now."

Sheriff Russell picked up the glass and held it out in a toast to Chopper, who still hung from the stag's antlers, like some perverse crucifixion scene.

"To Chopper." He said and took a swig, it burned his throat and he hissed through his teeth, "I'll get the bastard for you if it's the last thing I do."

CHAPTER 28

The snow had begun to fall heavier now and with night well and truly shrouding Maple Falls, the journey out of town towards the woods was a treacherous one. The Ford Lariat grumbled through the conditions, as cautiously as possible, even with those wheels chained it was much too dangerous to go picking up speed in these kinds of conditions.

"Can't you go any faster?" Agnes groaned as she leaned on the dashboard and peered through the clearing that the wiper was making as it sifted away the constant build up of snow, forcing it into a pile that rose up until it had nowhere to go and then fell away to the road.

"Will you quit asking that, Agnes!" Lieutenant Adams snapped, "The answer is still the same one that I've given you the last hundred times you've asked."

"Exaggeration much!" Agnes scoffed.
Adams just shook her head and peered through her own little window that her wiper was working so hard to keep clear.

The headlights cut through the darkness but at every turn seemed to be congested with thick falling flakes that did little to help them find their way.

They had followed the bloodied tracks of Beau Tooth's sledge at first, red lines in the snow became pink, then orange with flaking rust, then black with just the mud and dirt from underneath uncovered. It had been easy going before the snow had started to fall heavy and began to cover up the trail he left behind.

"If it continues to fall this heavy we will surely lose the trail." Adams sighed.

"Then we will have to go out on foot." Agnes declared.

"Are you crazy?" Adams scoffed, "If we do have to stop, then as an officer of the law I will be going out there, not you."

"To hell with that!" Agnes barked, "I want to see this bastard breathe his last breath. And if I have anything to do about it, I'll be the one to end his miserable fucking life."

"Agnes..." Adams sighed.

"Don't give me any of your patronising bullshit about upholding the law and doing it by the book!"

"I know you're angry, but normally..."

"Normally?" Agnes laughed, "There's nothing normal about this situation. Nothing normal about him! You've seen what he did, what he's done for the

261

past God knows how many years! He has to be stopped. Permanently!"

"And you're the one to do it are you?" Adams said with a scowl.

"Yeah, sure! Why not?"

Lieutenant Adams shook her head and sighed.

"There's no reasoning with the youth of today."

"Oh here we go!" Agnes folded her arms defiantly and rolled her eyes, "You're not my mother you know."

"Thank God!" Adams laughed, "I'd have put you over my knee a long time ago, I can tell you."

"Tut tut! You can't do that sort of thing these days Lieutenant. You should know that being an advocate for the law and all."

Adams turned her attention back to the road in front of her, not wanting to fall deeper into the rabbit hole of debating with Agnes, she knew it was an argument she could not hope to win. Agnes Duckworth would no doubt have an answer for any solution that she could suggest.

"Oh, the silent treatment now, huh?" Agnes scoffed but there was a playful smile on her bruised lips.

"Agnes!" Adams snapped, turning away from the windshield to glare at her.

"LOOK OUT!" Agnes squealed and grabbed the steering wheel and yanked it wildly.

The headlights flashed across a sledge packed with dead bodies, limbs protruding out at all angles as snow topped them, preserving them in a layer of ice.

The vehicle turned so suddenly that its wheels slid on the snow, unable to grip anything and went spilling down a bank at the side of the road and hurtling into a tree hood first.

Blackness came for a short time, Agnes didn't know how long, but when she came to there was another welt on her forehead and she groaned as she rubbed at it.

"Well at least we're in one piece." She said turning to Lieutenant Adams who was slumped over the steering wheel.

"No! Tammy!" She squealed and leaned her back in her seat, she was relieved to hear the Lieutenant grumble incoherently, but blood trickled down the bridge of her nose.

"I'm going to get some help." Agnes said and lifted up the radio transmitter, only to hear the trudging of heavy feet crunching through the snow, the sound drawing nearer and nearer. She leaned back in her seat and manoeuvred herself to see out of the rearview mirror. Tooth held his axe down by his side, dragging it through the snow as he approached the mangled vehicle.

"Mayday!" She whispered into the transmitter, "Help, fire, SOS! Fuck it I don't know what to say!"

Tooth got nearer and then the sound of crunching snow stopped and all there was, was the sound of the wind whistling in the night.

"He's here!" She gasped and grasping the receiver in her grip she cried into it, "Somebody... anybody send help! We have crashed somewhere off the Maple Cross and..."

The line went dead and just a hissing of static could be heard. She tried to fiddle with the radio dials but was met by nothingness.

"Shit." She hissed.

She turned to Adams and shook her by her shoulders.

"Wake up Tammy! Shit, he's here!"

But Tammy remained unconscious, oblivious to the peril that they had found themselves in.

Agnes reached for the Lieutenant's side arm and held it in her hands, spinning in her seat to face the rear window of the vehicle, but he wasn't there. She looked around each side, but all she saw was darkness and snow, one headlight still flickered outside, but did little to help her see anything.

Suddenly the vehicle moved, its chassis dipping, the wheel arches almost scrapping on the chains wrapped around the rear tyres. It was as if the vehicle had taken on extra weight.

264

It had.

The metal creaked with each movement as Beau Tooth made his way onto the roof of the vehicle. Agnes heard the scrapping of the axe on the metal of the car and she sat gazing up in the darkness at the ceiling of the vehicle.

She held her breath for the longest time, but there was nothingness, it was silent apart from that chilling wind outside. She clasped the gun tightly in her hands holding it close like a comfort blanket, waiting for the inevitable.

She waited for what felt like a lifetime and the radio burst into a loud screech of static that made her jump and she could hear the voice of Sheriff Russell on the other end.

"Agnes? Agnes is that you? Where are you?"

But as she reached to take the transmitter from its holster there was a huge thumping sound coming from the roof and the axe made its way through the ceiling and swept past her face.

She screamed loudly and tried to scramble out of her seat belt and again the axe cut through the roof like a knife through cheddar and swirled past her like a lethal pendulum. The axe head burst through the perspex glass that sat behind the front seats to protect officer's from perpetrators that found themselves in the rear of the vehicles. She unleashed the bullets from the gun.

Six shots plowed through windows and the shredded roof, but she couldn't be sure whether they hit anything.

For a moment her head was filled to the brim with hope as there was silence and the axe had ceased its swiping at her. She undid the seatbelt and again shook Adams trying to wake her. She failed in her attempt again and undid the Lieutenant's seatbelt and manoeuvred her down low in her seat as to not be hit by any further axe attacks. It was only by pure perverse luck that Adams hadn't been split in half by the swiping of Tooth's axe.

But the axe came again and buried itself into the spongy headrest of where Lieutenant Adams had just sat. Agnes screamed again and the axe continued to carve up the roof until she could see him now glaring down at her. She tried her door but it wouldn't open, the impact of the tree had caused the front of the vehicle to bend around the hinge of the door and forbade it from opening.

"Shit, shit! Fucking door! Argh!" She growled, each attempt to open the door was a failure, then the axe collided with the back of her head and she saw stars, lucky for her it was but a glancing blow and did not break the skin, but already she could feel the lump rising up on top of her head. His hand came through the hole in the roof next and grabbed at her, it curled around her dark curls and threatened to rip each one from her scalp if she did not comply.

She reached forward for anything that she could use to release his grip, but found nothing of any use. She grabbed her bag and began opening it looking for the flare gun, but Tooth gave a hard yank and pulled her up out of her seat banging her head against a portion of the roof that still remained intact. She reached forward again and pushed in the cigarette lighter, but all she could do was wait. She fought as well as she could until a wedge of her hair came loose and found itself wrapped around Tooth's blackened fingers.

Agnes squealed with pain as her hairless scalp began to bleed and as she leaned over to try Adams' door she found that it was jammed too.

"Oh God, no!" She seethed as she frantically yanked the door handle to no avail.

His hand was through again reaching and it grabbed the hood of her sweater and yanked it, almost pulling it up over her head. She heard the pop of the cigarette lighter announce that it was ready and she reached for it pulling it out and pressing it tightly to the thick, meaty forearm of Beau Tooth.

"Take that you fuck!" She seethed victoriously, but nothing seemed to happen, the lighter was glowing red with its heat and it seeped through the flesh and Agnes could not understand why it wasn't hurting him.

She was not to know that the layers of flesh he wore were not his own. It was quite possible that she was forcing that poker of heat through her own deceased brother's flesh.

Finally he gave out a growl of bitterness and let go of her as he fished the lighter out of his forearm, obviously the heat had found the beast within.

Before she could think of her next move he had jumped down onto the twisted hood of the car and drove the axe through the windshield. She screamed again and clambered over the backseats, the broken shards of perspex glass tore at her clothes and she was suddenly halted. Tooth was peering in through the broken windshield with his hand wrapped around her ankle, she managed to kick him off and she fell into the rear of the vehicle and thankfully the rear door was open, she dropped out into the snow and clambered back up the bank. Tooth growled angrily and jumped down from the vehicle and gave chase.

Agnes reached the road and ran straight into the sledge, the faces of the freezing dead gazed up at her with pleading eyes and she squealed, before turning to see Tooth trudging up the bank.

She did the only thing she could think of and that was to run into the cover of woods.

CHAPTER 29

Sheriff Russell staggered out of Chopper's just like he had done many times before over the past twelve months, but this time was different. He had not drunken himself into a stupor to forget about the mess his marriage had become or to numb the pain he felt from the guilt of not being able to save those that fell to Beau Tooth' axe. No, this exit from the bar had left him shaken, the blood stained floorboards and his good friend hanging from the wall, mutilated and displayed like some trophy had been too much for him to take. He leaned up against the frame of the door and heaved, the tendons in his neck pulled taut as he threatened to vomit, luckily for him the vomit refused to leave and instead he was left with a twisted knot in his gut and a sore throat from the retching.

Nora approached him and nuzzled his hand, he gave her a haphazard stroke and then seemed to drift away, the dog seemed to catch the scent of something untoward and scampered away from the bar to seek refuge in the alleyway at the side of the building.

He let the cold night air caress his face, it soothed him and for a moment he felt content, almost happy, the feeling was so delicate that it almost made him forget everything as he closed his eyes and let snowflakes settle on his cheeks.

Reality hit home soon enough as his nostrils started to twitch frantically, his brow furrowed and his face contorted with displeasure as though he had trodden in something unseemly and unleashed the stench it held within. The smell was blood and death, darkness and decay and he was forced to open his eyes.

Even though he could have very easily stayed in that darkness for the rest of his life, content, not needing to deal with what was happening in the real world, he was forced to open his eyes.

He wished he hadn't. He wished he had gone with his first instinct and remained in the darkness behind the safety of his eyelids, but he was unable to do so.

"Good God!" He gasped and fell against the door frame, his head swimming, he was thankful that the door frame was there because it was the only thing propping him upright.

He gazed into the wide eyes of Wendy Hardwood.

Pain and fear were captured at her final moments her head left her body and were displayed for all to see how her final moments on the mortal coil felt.

"Oh my dearest, Wendy..." He whispered as he staggered away from her and out onto the road not able to look at her anymore.

He stood in the middle of the high street and turned around slowly taking in all of the carnage that had been left behind. The pure shit that had been left by Beau Tooth for him to clean up once again.

"I can't allow this to continue to happen." He seethed, teeth gritted and fists clenched, "I will not allow the people of this town to be treated this way."

There was the sound of scraping metal and the overturned Ford Lariat's door slowly worked its way open and Sergeant Church crawled out into the snow.

"Emily!" Cried, Sheriff Russell moving quickly to her aid and helped her up.

"Sheriff, I mean this with all the respect in the world, but what the fuck is going on in this town?"

The Sheriff actually smirked, not at the situation but the fact that Sergeant Church could still keep her sense of humour even in such dark times.

"I thought you were as good as dead."

"I feel like it." She said cringing as she stretched out her back, "I probably should be."

"Is somebody going to get me the hell out of here?" Came the distressed cries of Officer Smith who was still caught upside down, attached by the seat belt and visibly distraught.

271

"Smith?" Sheriff Russell said, leaning over to see him.

"Oh! Hi Sheriff!" Officer Smith glowed with embarrassment and tried to salute him.

"Okay, okay, keep your badge on!" Sergeant Church scoffed, with an impatient roll of her eyes.

"Right I need you two to cordon off the area and touch base with the locals. Tell them there is nothing to fear, but to stay in their homes."

"And is there? Truly?" The Sergeant asked.

"What?"

"Is there truly nothing to fear?"

The Sheriff sighed and gazed around, his eyes followed the trail lines that were already being smothered with a new layer of snow.

"I hope so...I think he's done for the winter."

"I should hope so!" She scoffed, "You wouldn't have believed how many bodies he had piled up on that sledge of his."

"All we can do is stop him from adding anymore."

"Tell me you're not going after him?" Church gasped.

"I have to do my duty, Sergeant."

"But..."

"And you need to do yours." He snapped, not allowing her to finish her sentence.

"Yes, Sir. I understand."

"Bruce Hardwood will need cutting down from the inside of the bar."

"Are you serious?"

"Unfortunately, yes I am. He's been left as yet another trophy on Chopper's hunting wall."

"The sick bastard!" She growled. "Why did he leave him? I mean, he's taken all the other bodies, right?"

The Sheriff pondered this for a moment and hadn't thought of it that way, but believed that it was personal.

"As a message."

"A message? To whom?"

To me.

"To the people of Maple Falls that he will be back."

"Please get me out of here." Groaned Office Smith, "Things are aching that I didn't know could ache."

"Oh, quit complaining!" Church snapped.

"Did anyone see where Agnes Duckworth went?"

"Who?" Sergeant Church said with a shrug.

"The girl I was with. She was the sister of one of those that went missing from the cabins last year."

"Oh, she left with Lieutenant Adams, Sheriff." Smith said from upside down in the vehicle.

"At least she's safe." Sheriff Russell sighed with relief.

"Erm, not really." Smith said.

"What do you mean? Surely Tammy would have taken her back to the office, or got her out of town?"

"I'm afraid not, Sheriff. They took off after the guy with the axe and his sledge full of bodies."

"No!" He seethed, "Shit!"

"We can come with you, Sheriff." Sergeant Church said.

"No, you'll be needed here." He started to walk away with purpose following the trail of sledge tracks out of town, "Get every able officer in now to help you clean this place up. Fire service too. Anybody that can help. Keep your sidearm at the ready and make sure the locals stay indoors."

"Yes, Sheriff." Church said and marched off towards *Chopper's Bar* as she called in her superior's orders on her radio.

"What about me, damn it?" Smith groaned, he sighed and undid the clip on the seat belt and collapsed unceremoniously into a pile on the ceiling of the upturned vehicle.

Sheriff Russell picked up speed to a jog and whistled for Nora to join him, she did and matched his stride with purpose, she was enjoying her newfound career as a police dog.

274

"We need a bit of luck on our side, Nora, that's what we need." He said panting as he hit Maple Cross. There was a loud blast of a truck horn and he turned to see the gigantic yellow snow plough rumbling up the road behind him.

"Good old Mack!" Russell chuckled and stood in the knee deep snow as the lights of the machine bathed him and he waved his hands to signal the driver to stop. The snow plough slowed down to a halt, the front plough that was cutting through the snow sending it left and right like raging waves, slowed and the snow settled in front of it calm as a water on a lake.

The window was wound down and a grizzled looking man with a knitted wooden hat peered through the window, a half chewed cigar hanging from the corner of his mouth.

"Is that you, Sheriff?" Mack asked.

"It sure is, Mack."

"What in the name of Mike are you doing out here? Hey, is that Eddie's dog?"

"I'll explain on the way. Can I get a lift?"

"Hop in Sheriff. Late night ploughing is fun and all but it doesn't half get lonely. I'd be glad of the company."

Sheriff Russell scaled the ladder and joined Mack in the cab and Nora jumped up after him joining him on his lap as the snow plough moved out once again and turned the calm sea of whiteness that lay ahead into a frenzy as it cut through it.

CHAPTER 30

The sound of Agnes's laboured breaths seeped into the surrounding mass of trees, reverberating off the twisted trunks of all manner of different trees. The lodgepole pines, the thick solid presence of the dormant spruces, maples and red oaks crowded around her, almost suffocating her. The sound came back to meet her ears, the feeling that someone was hot on her heels, breathing down her neck, saliva dripping down her spine and causing anxiety-ridden goosebumps to rise up and devour her flesh. She had tried so hard not to turn around for fear that Tooth was so close.

She couldn't bring herself to look over her shoulder in case he was there, toying with her, waiting for her to turn around and notice him so that he had the satisfaction of looking into her eyes and seeing her fear as he took his axe and sliced through her throat. Instead she made her way through the surrounding trees hoping that they would act as cover, praying that she would become lost behind their wide hardened trunks. But the trees seemed to be against her, it was as if the woods were teaming up on her and willing the brute to catch up so they could witness him having his way with her and laugh at the outcome. Several times the trembling Aspen trees had appeared from nowhere, bark so pale it became one with the winter scene that surrounded her, seeing them too late she had run into them or tripped over their roots.

Even when she would seek comfort behind a fir or hemlock, her back pressed up against the coarse bark, trying so hard to stop the rapid beating of her heart and the gasping wheeze of her fatigued breaths, but whenever she took a moment, she could hear his heavy footfalls echoing through the woods, constant and purposeful, closing in on her with each second that ticked away.

Her warming breath led the way, a plume bursting forward as if guiding her way in the darkness, the snow had halted for the time being and she gazed upwards to the navy sky above, clear of clouds and full of stars, the moon beckoning to her upwards.

She tried to remember the last time she had seen the moon, since arriving in Maple Falls the sky had been so congested with the constant thick, denseness of the nimbostratus clouds that she had forgotten what the moon looked like.

She did what she was asked subconsciously, climbing a slight hill that turned into a steeper ascent, before she knew it there was rock under her feet, her bosom now flat against a mountain wall as she clung on for dear life with ice cold fingertips.

Climbing out onto a ledge she thought she was safe but as she looked back down the craggy rock face she could see his hulking, menacing shadow making the ascent. It seemed easier for him, one with the wilderness and the knowledge of easier routes which meant less climbing saw him make good speed.

"Damn it!" She murmured, "He is relentless."

She gazed out at the view, in the darkness it was a mass of tree tops and mountain peaks, its beauty subdued by the darkness, but the moon and stars shone wildly and picked out the peaks allowing them to shimmer like blades piercing the sky, looking to slice it open and unleash a fresh wave of snow.

She turned back and could hear the falling of rubble, she leaned over the ledge and the cold wind caressed her face, sweeping her hair back and pricking the wounds and bruises that were cut into her flesh. She hoped that the falling of rubble was Tooth losing his grip and plummeting to his death on the rocks below.

She was wrong, even with one hand clasping his axe he still found it easier to climb upwards than she had.

"I need to move on or he will be on me." She said to herself and looked around, perhaps she could hide in one of the crevices that was cut into the rock face. But the fear of getting stuck there and being a sitting duck moved her train of thought away from such things and she climbed higher still to another ledge.

She scrambled upwards, lost her footing and rubble became dislodged and cascaded down the rock face, she grabbed hold of a protruding rock and hung there for a moment as she screamed loudly into the night. The echo swept around her with the breeze, it sounded as though it was mocking her and she knew that somewhere down below Beau Tooth was smiling, salivating.

Agnes managed to climb up onto the ledge and lay on her back breathing heavily as she looked up at the moon that looked almost translucent. On the outskirts of the mountains she saw those dreaded clouds closing in again and she knew that more snow was on the way.

Somewhere in the woods a dog barked, the sound carried and it got her attention and her moist eyes slid back down toward the mass of trees below. Her eyes widened suddenly as the beam of a flashlight erupted through the gloom, passing slowly from one side of the wood to the other like the turning of a light in a lighthouse.

She sat up and a smile appeared on her doughy face, almost overwhelmed by elation she wanted to cry and laugh at the same time.

Then she heard his voice, the gravelly, caring tone of Sheriff Russell as he called her name.

"It's the Sheriff!" She gasped.

Quickly she slipped her rucksack off her back and rummaged through it, finding the flare gun once again, holding it in her hands and aiming it skyward.

"I'll let him know where I am." She said with excitement in her tone that suddenly turned to caution, "No! I only have one flare and if it hit the rocks it could cause an avalanche."

She slid the flare gun back into her rucksack and flung it back onto her back as she stood up. The cold air rippled against her, she was feeling the effects of the conditions now, wearing only a hooded sweatshirt, she hugged herself tightly.

"I can't stay here, I have to move." She said, she knew she had to move or Tooth would be on her. She did what she thought was right and called back to the Sheriff, informing him of her whereabouts.

The flashlight beam thrashed around from side to side and then the beam hit the mountain face and she heard him reply, it was a muffled reply that sounded like he said he was coming, and to stay where she was. But there was no way she could do that, not with Tooth on her trail, by the time the Sheriff reached her it would be no doubt too late. When she saw the flashlight below her and pointed at the rock face and adamant that he was on the right track, she moved upwards again making it onto a wider ledge that stretched out to give her more space, she disappeared around a corner and found a cave, it was wide and dark within and that sent a shudder down her spine. She wasn't brave enough to enter, part of her didn't know what she was afraid of, surely there couldn't be anything more terrifying than what was chasing her. But even still she decided that she would hide in a crevice near the cave and hope that Tooth would believe that she would have sought refuge within its dark maw.

CHAPTER 31

"That's it Nora, good girl." Sheriff Russell praised as he started to climb the steep hill.

When he had arrived on the outskirts of Maple Woods and saw Lieutenant Adams' 4x4 wrapped around a tree at the bottom of a bank he had feared the worst. He had clambered down the snow covered bank as Mack watched on in disbelief. The vehicle had been totalled but not just because of the crash, windows had been put through and the roof was a mangled sculpture of twisted steel. It had been torn open by some sharp instrument.

"An axe." He had murmured to himself, the scene had pulled him back to a year ago and the roof looked very much like the 1983 Vandura cargo van that had been found at the lumberjack cabins.

"Found anything, Sheriff?" Mack had shouted and it had pulled him back from his reverie.

"No, nothing yet." He replied moving in closer and shining a flashlight inside the vehicle. In the driver's seat he noticed a slumped body, covered in blood and snowflakes.

"Tammy!" He had gasped and tried with all his might to open the door to get to her but it refused to budge. He had been frantic and swept round to the rear of the car which was open and retrieved a crowbar before returning and jamming it into the crease where the door met the frame.

"Is everything okay down there?" Mack had called.

"I've found Tammy!" The Sheriff had called back, sweat on his brow as he moved his weight into the crowbar to prise open the door.

"Is she..." Mack said and then stopped himself, clapping his hand over his mouth as Nora sat next to him.

"I hope not." The Sheriff murmured to himself through gritted teeth, he knew the end of Mack's sentence and he didn't like it one bit.

The door burst open and he hoisted her up into his arms, she seemed to weigh nothing and everything all at once, the burden of whether she was okay was the heaviest weight he had ever felt. Then she groaned and the weight seemed to lift.

"She's gonna be okay." He called to Mack who had come down to help carry her back up to the bank.

284

Mack had taken her back to the Sheriff's Office on strict instructions to wait with her until she felt okay to be left.

Now he found himself trudging up a steep hill, with the jagged point of a mountain his destination.

Nora yowled loudly when she had heard the girl call from the rock face and she had danced in the snow, she had been right to listen to her instincts and her barks were a smug message to the Sheriff that she should have been trusted all along.

The sheepdog had run past the sledge that was stacked with bodies, perhaps she couldn't bear to be faced with her loved one's dead face. The look of Eddie Gotch's eyes encased in fear would have broken her little heart. Even Sheriff Russell had not taken the time to survey who was on that sledge, he saw the faces of those he knew and knew well and followed the dog at speed, even he couldn't face that, not yet.

Nora had been able to maintain the scent even through the wintery conditions, the tracks were easier to follow granted, but there were discrepancies with the trail they were following, some even led to dead ends behind trees.

"Clever Girl." Sheriff Russell had said with a smirk even if it was a dead end and nothing came of it, because he knew that she was trying to confuse Beau Tooth, to lead him on a wild goose chase while she made her escape. But good old Nora was not to be deceived by the detours, she remained loyal to her instincts and was vocal enough to tell Sheriff Russell he was searching in the wrong place. Nora had danced around the foot of the steep hill that led to a mountain face, kicking up the snow with her paws and nuzzling her nose deep underneath the layer of cracked ice and snow revelling in the scent.

The Sheriff shone the flashlight upwards as he made his ascent, the beam of light caught the shape of a hulking silhouette who walked the ledges leading ever upwards. Tooth was not built for climbing mountains and although the walking of the ledges would obviously take him longer, it was safer and he knew that the girl had nowhere to go. His prey was defenceless and cornered and that was just how he liked it.

"This is a big mistake, Agnes." The Sheriff said to himself or Nora if she was listening, "She'll be cornered up there with nowhere to go but down."

He shook away the thought of her plummeting from the mountain, her body breaking across the mass of boulders and rocks that gathered at its foot, like hungry sharks who smell blood, waiting patiently in the calm icy waters below.

"I hope she knows what she's doing."

Nora had started to slide backwards, unable to reach the rocky section of the mountain. The Sheriff stopped and knelt by her, she was whining and was frantic, stubbornly she continued to try and reach the next level, if she could then it would be plain sailing for her without the mass of snow to slow her down.

"I think you've come to the end of the line." He stroked her and her eyes were sad as if she was upset that she could no longer be of assistance. He stroked her lovingly and she nuzzled at his neck.
But he rose and continued on his way.

"Wait for me, Nora." He said and she sat in the snow, her ears and eyes drooping with sadness as she pined for him.

"I'll be right back." He said and then cursed his stupidity at such an outrageous comment.
If I survive the climb. If I don't fall to my death. If I'm not decapitated by some insane axe wielding maniac, yeah then I'll be right back. Stupid!
He only looked back once and could already see that the dog looked anxious, but he had to concentrate on the matter in hand and made it up to the first ledge and the rocky terrain, disappearing out of the dog's sight. Nora sniffed at the air, all the scents that surrounded her made her anxious, there were other horrors in these woods that would believe she was easy prey sitting here like this. The aromas that she knew of were cougars and bears, moose and raccoon. The scents of blood and death that belonged to the man with the axe.

The stale stench of body odour and whiskey of Sheriff Russell, she actually liked the scent it was calming as it reminded her of Eddie Gotch. The smell of fear which she attributed to the girl and there was something else down here with her, a scent she had never experienced before, like thick damp fur and moss, she didn't like it and she wasn't about to sit there and be taken unaware. She continued to run up the hill and jump to the rocky level, she wouldn't stop because her Sheriff needed her help.

CHAPTER 32

The wind howled into a frenzy and spiralled around the jagged rocks of the mountain face. Agnes stood shivering in a crevice near an entrance to a cave. She gazed up and could not see the top of the mountain, the snow capped peak disappeared into a world of cloud that had moved in to smother that navy sky, ignoring the stars and threatening to erase the moon. She swallowed hard, the moon was her only source of light.

"Don't put me in the dark." She began to cry, "I couldn't take it if I was in the dark."

She suddenly stuffed her hands into her pockets and searched for her cellphone. With no luck, she did the same with her oversized hooded sweatshirt, but the result was the same.

"Shit." She hissed, as she checked her rucksack, knowing all the while that it had been in the pocket of her parka that met the flames bursting from a Volkswagen Beetle and was now a twisted piece of plastic and of no use to anyone.

She pulled her hood up over her head and wrapped her arms around her bosom, as she slowly slid down the wall wedging herself in tightly of the hollow nook and prayed that it would keep her out of sight.

"The Sheriff is coming for you." She told herself, "Just sit tight, help is coming."

She swallowed hard on those words, really trying to believe them, swallowed them so hard that they nearly choked her. She knew deep down that she couldn't be certain, not really. What she was certain of was that Beau Tooth was coming for her, it was all a matter of who reached her first.

The wind whistled a sinister tune as it passed through the crevice, she lifted her rucksack and clutched it tightly to her, sniffing at its scent of stale cigarettes and cat hair, the smells of home. It may not have been to anyone else's tastes, but to her it was comforting and she closed her eyes and drifted away on that cold wind, hoping that she would wake up from it.

"What was that?" She gasped as she woke from her slumber. She couldn't say for sure how long she had slept but it was snowing heavily now and a layer rested upon her shoulders. As she moved her head to peer through the crack in the rocks, she disturbed flecks of ice and snow that had settled in her hair.

Whatever sound had stirred her was not in effect now, just the wailing shrieks of wind that brought with it yet another snow storm.

She looked around the clearing and the cave. From where she was there seemed to be no change out there, the wind swept into the mouth of the cave and it sounded like a monstrous growl as if to warn off any stragglers wishing to seek cover from the storm.

Agnes stood up slowly and as quietly as she could, she slid with her back against rock to the opening of this jagged gap in the rock face.

She saw nothing, so she bravely sidestepped closer and closer to the entrance of her hiding place. She gazed out at the cave and a flurry of snow swept across the undisturbed layer that carpeted the ledge. She sighed with relief, by now the brute may well have passed her by and his search could have led him around the ledge to the other side of the mountain or perhaps into the cave. She believed that this was her moment to make her escape, if Tooth had passed her or was seeking refuge in the cave then she believed that she could quietly slip back down the mountain and back to town. She sighed heavily and a plume of breath erupted into the night sky, duelling with the delicate flakes of falling snow.

"You're a coward, Agnes Duckworth." She whispered, "A fucking coward! You came back out here to end this bastard! Now you want to run back to town with your tail between your legs."

As she attempted to step out from her hiding place she was immediately frozen in mid motion as a cloud of stale smelling breath exploded in front of her and the massive bulk of Beau Tooth trudged right past her. Her eyes grew wide, magnified by her glasses. She looked like some frightened owl, she didn't move, she didn't breathe she didn't dare. But she watched on as he marched towards the cave entrance. She slowly slid back into her nook and peered out through a frame of rock and a curtain of falling snow. Her eyes were only for the gargantuan beast that stood motionless in the snow. His axe slid down in his grip and the head collided with the rock below, the sound of it sang out and carried around the mountain. Tooth stood motionless, seemingly unaffected by the conditions that spiralled around him, the same weather that caused a quiver across Agnes's flesh and chilled her to the bone, her body trembling uncontrollably.

"Agnes!" Gasped Sheriff Russell as he continued his ascent, he had lost his ushanka that had warmed his head so nicely, but after nearly taking a spill off the side of the mountain he was glad it was the hat and not him.

"I'm coming, Agnes, hang on in there." He grimaced as he climbed and was met by a fresh sweeping of snow that blinded him for a moment causing him to lose his footing and leave him hanging unceremoniously by one hand for several seconds. He clawed at the rocks frantically before regaining his composure and pulling himself up to safety.

He lay for a time and let the snow fill the contours of his gaunt face, but then a sound erupted from above, the vicious sound of steel on rock.

"Agnes, no!" He grimaced and he rose to his feet and headed along the ledge upwards toward the sound of a reaper's scythe preparing itself to take another soul.

"Why doesn't he move?" Agnes hissed.

As if he heard her words the brute moved towards the cave, boots sweeping through the snow and the axe head dragging along the surface creating a shrilling shriek that took to the air to ride the wind around and around in a haunting spiral.

Tooth disappeared into the cave and was eaten up by the darkness within.

Agnes immediately shuffled towards her exit again and stepped out onto the wide ledge once more. She gazed at her feet as they left a footprint in the snow and then her eyes flitted to Tooth's prints and swallowed hard, his prints quadruped her dainty size 6's and it was enough to send another shiver down her spine as she turned away from the cave and attempted to make her escape.

Coward.

The word hit her in her spleen and caused her to stop, the word came on the wind she believed but it was her own subconscious she knew.

"Don't do this. Not now." She growled, "This is not the time to have a fight with my own morality."

She took a few steps away again in the direction that would lead her to safety and then was halted again.

"Why did you come here?" She asked herself, "You came to find out what happened to Chester and now why are you standing in the snow, half way up a fucking mountain freezing your lips off."

She looked up at the moon that appeared from behind a mass of clouds and she sighed heavily.

"You came for vengeance!" She said and turned to face the cave just as the clouds swept across the moon again and brought with it yet another flurry of snow.

"You can't let Chester down. He was your brother goddamn it and he deserves some justice."

She dropped her rucksack to the floor and took out a photograph of her brother, Chester, or Quack to his friends and watched as it took on snowflakes and she wiped them away like tears and kissed it before sliding it into her pants pocket.

"I won't let your death be in vain." She said and then retrieved the flare gun, this time making sure that the safety catch was not slid into place to hamper her.

She turned around and saw the cave behind the gloom and a shower of fresh snowflakes, until the moon appeared again and brightened up the ledge.

The twinkle of Tooth's axe was the first thing she saw as it reflected the smile of the moon and it took her aback.

"No." She whimpered, but held the flare gun out towards him as he emerged into the light, a grin as big and as sharp as the one gazing down at her from the night sky.

"Not this time!" She growled and aimed, her finger quivered over the trigger, the snow swept across and obscured her view and when it swept past again, she realised that he had moved towards her slightly and then stopped.

"I'm not playing your fucking games any longer!"

She did not fire, she was terrified to miss, knowing that she only had one shot and the falling snow and wind made it difficult to see.

"I'm not going to run away from you, not again, not anymore!"

She shielded her face again from the snow and when she looked again he was closer still.

"No, no, no." She cried as the flare gun slipped from her grip and into the snow.

She searched for it, found it and gripped the handle tightly, she winced from the discomfort of her dislocated or broken fingers, before standing up and spinning around in the snow believing that Tooth would be there in front of her ready to take her head. But there was nothing, just the empty mouth of the cave and the falling snow.

"What?" She gasped, aiming the flare gun into the snow at several places, but he had disappeared.

"Agnes!" A voice came from behind her and a hand seized her shoulder.

She screamed and spun around striking Sheriff Russell in the face with the flare gun. It floored him and drew blood from his temple as he lay in the snow unconscious.

"Shit! Sheriff, oh shit what have I done now?" She cried and she knelt by his side and slapped at his face gently trying to bring him round again.

Suddenly her attention was drawn above her as her scream still lingered around the peak of the mountain and a flurry of rocks and snow cascaded down from above and collided with the ledge near the opening of the cave.

"Avalanche!" She stood up quickly and her whole body tensed and hoped that it was just a warning. After several long seconds it subsided and she breathed a sigh of relief. She turned around to see the floored Sheriff and was met by a hand around her throat as the thick meaty grip of Beau Tooth clasped around her whole neck and began to squeeze.

Agnes let go of the flare gun and heard its hard plastic shell collide with the rocky terrain hidden under a fresh layer of fine snow.

She gave up the struggle immediately and allowed her arms to fall by her side, her legs didn't kick and went limp, toes of her shoes pointing down towards the disturbed snow below. She had given up the fight, she had nothing more inside her to cope with this beast's insatiable appetite for death and destruction. Her face was slowly turning several shades, her plump cheeks now resembling bruised peaches and her lips were narrowing and bluish. Tooth pulled her in closer, the stench from his breath was maddening as it besieged her nostrils and she could do nothing about it.

He smiled as he removed her glasses and threw them into a pile of snow, he stared into her eyes as if in search of something. His head tilted to one side for a moment as if he had found what he was looking for, it was an odd look that caressed his brow, but who knew what Beau Tooth was thinking? Agnes coughed and cackled, saliva swimming in the back of her throat and it brought Tooth back to the moment in hand, instinctively grimacing and throttling her harder still.

Her eyes bulged and began to leak with tears that ran down her swollen face, as if he was squeezing the juice from a citrus fruit. As the snow and tears fell, she remembered everything, her life passing before her within the fall of a tear, it made her smile, but inevitably there was only death that remained and the last thing she would see was blood, as a crimson dome was lowered over her world of white.

There was the sound of several muffled gunshots that reverberated around her and the grip that held her so tightly, suddenly loosened and released her allowing her to fall to the ground, her head swimming with flurries of white and red above her. The blood vessel in her left eye had burst, turning its sclera a bright red.

Through blurred vision of blood and snow she saw Tooth favouring his left forearm as blood spurted from a wound, he growled and spun around to see Sheriff Russell standing up holding his revolver out in front of him.

Tooth seemed to be shook and gazed around looking for his axe that he had left discarded in the snow when he had attacked Agnes.

"I don't believe it." Russell gasped, with a shake of his head as he looked upon the brute that had terrorised Maple Falls for so many years. He had put three bullets into the monster, but only one had done any damage and it actually pleased him to see that blood was trickling from his forearm, belief in the knowledge that he was human after all and if he bleeds then he could die too.

Tooth found the axe and lifted it out of the snow, Agnes sleepily grabbed the axe to halt Tooth's progress, but he yanked it away from her and she fell into the snow, her head still spinning as her lungs yearned for air.

The pair stood watching each other, Sheriff Russell actually smirking at the brute, it may well have been this odd demeanour that stalled Tooth's attack, not many victims had met him and smiled at him, it disturbed him somewhat.

"I was beginning to think that I was going mad, you know." Russell scoffed, "I was starting to believe the folks in town as they called me insane and a part of me never really believed that you existed, not truly."

Tooth manoeuvred the axe in front of him and spun its head around in his hands masterfully, but his discoloured eyes never left the Sheriff's.

The pair began to circle each other, feet shuffling sideways in the snow, Sheriff Russell refusing to drop his firearm or his gaze, his foot trod on Agnes's rucksack and then kicked against the flare gun.

Tooth circled too, allowing the axehead to fall into the snow and he dragged it across the rock beneath as he

299

moved, his heavy boot found Agnes's glasses and the sound of broken glass and plastic echoed around them. As the wind picked up, so did the snow, the flurry of flakes swirling around the pair before Russell found Agnes with his foot and stopped, standing over her like some guardian.

"Are you okay, Agnes?" He asked.

She groaned back at him incoherently.

"Come on girl, let me know you're okay." He asked again, but his eyes refused to leave Beau Tooth's.

"H-He broke my glasses...they were...my...only pair."

"I'll buy you a new pair! Just stay with me."

The amount of sweat that cascaded from his hairline was alarming, fear was reaching out and grasping him by his limbs and digging in its sharp claws of anxiety and he felt it. It was having the desired effect and the revolver in his hands began to quiver.

Beau Tooth, ever the hunter, noticed this change in demeanour immediately and gave a little grin to let the Sheriff know that he knew.

"W-What?" Sheriff stuttered, "You think I'm scared of you?"

Beau Tooth gripped the axe in both hands and growled.

"Of course I'm scared of you! I'm fucking terrified!"

Tooth smiled and licked at his chapped lips, this was music to his ears.

"But do you know something?" Russell chuckled before screaming, "YOU'VE RUINED MY LIFE!"
The rocks from above trembled under his painful wail and several pieces of rubble worked their way free and fell down around them.

"Because of you I have lost everything. Honour, respect, my identity. But above all, love! All because of you."
Tooth grew tired of the man's words and playfully took a swing with the axe at his revolver, it swept past and cut through the snow, missing the muzzle by a hair, but it was enough to make Sheriff Russell flinch and step backwards, almost tripping over Agnes's leg.
Tooth attacked, but the Sheriff still had his wits about him and was quick to unleash the rest of the bullets that were waiting eagerly in the chambers of his revolver.
One bullet ricocheted off the axe head and was sent hurtling out into the wilderness somewhere. Tooth was moving forward now with purpose and he took another swipe with the axe that caused Russell to duck and then fall into the snow. Tooth stalking him but even on his backside, the Sheriff unleashed another bullet that stripped his thigh of some of its denim and then Tooth was on him, axe coming down in a furious strike.

Sheriff Russell had enough wits about him to roll out of the way and let the axe bite down on the rock. Chips of rock splintered into the air to join the snow and Tooth turned slowly to meet a bullet in the throat. Blood splattered out from the wound as the bullet cut through flesh and tendon and then lodged itself into the rock face. Tooth dropped the axe and instinctively grabbed his neck, the blood seeped through his fingers but he smiled back at the Sheriff who sighed back, knowing that the injury was not a killing one and in a few moments the blood wound clot and protect the wound.

"Now you have even taken satisfaction from me." Russell sighed, his revolver limp and useless in his hands and as Tooth's bloodied hand gripped around the Sheriff's throat, the revolver fell to the floor.

Agnes staggered to her feet and grabbed the flare gun and aimed it at Tooth.

"No..." She screamed, but the sound was cut off by Tooth's other hand around her throat.

He held them both gasping for air, in total control of them both, lifeless puppets on his strings. Agnes dropped the flare gun once again, no fight left, limbs useless and limp. Russell still had fight left in him and he kicked and punched at nothing, but his eyes watered and they found Agnes's glassy gaze.

"I-I'm...S-Sorry..." He hacked and coughed as he looked into her swollen face, "...I...f-failed...every...one."

There was a howl that erupted around them and a vicious growl as Nora burst through the falling snow and attacked Tooth. Nora bit down hard on his wrist and he was forced to release the Sheriff who collapsed to the ground holding his throat and gasping for air, tasting the snow on his lips and tongue was like being born again.

Tooth shook away Nora who landed back on her feet and bared her teeth, blood staining them pink and frothing in a frenzy in the corner of her jowls. She charged him again, jaws open and reaching up for his throat but Tooth swatted her away. He dropped Agnes in a pile of snow and turned his full attention to Nora who came again and gnawed at his meaty thigh. Tooth kicked the dog away and she collided with the rock face and with a yelp fell in a motionless pile in the snow.

Russell growled in a frenzy and launched himself at the brute landing punches that felt as though he was striking a bag of sand and having now effect on him. This time both Tooth's hands were around his throat as if to make sure this time to kill him quickly, but Russell refused to go without a fight and feeling around on the monster's thick forearms he found the gaping hole where the bullet was still lodged and sunk his finger

303

into the wound. The tip of his finger met the cool shell of the bullet and he pushed with all his might. Beau Tooth let out a painful cry and let go of the Sheriff, staggering backwards away from him grasping his forearm in his hand. The wail was animalistic in its tone and reverberated around the rock face, causing more snow and rubble to fall around him, the horrendous sound like some wild war cry.

Tooth's breaths were laboured now and his eyes were burning with hatred as he focused on the Sheriff who stood defiantly in front of him. As the sound of his cry was finally swept away on the wind there was a pause and Tooth took a step towards the Sheriff only to be halted by a similar sound erupting from within the cave. Sheriff Russell's eyes widened and he took several steps backwards as Tooth turned slowly to gaze upon a huge grizzly bear that lumbered out from the cave on its hind legs, towering over Tooth and roaring at him, saliva hanging from his jowls in thick strands, burning eyes of annoyance for having his winter sleep interrupted.

"There's always a bigger fish my friend." Said Patrick Russell as Tooth collided with the gigantic bear. The colossal tussle between the bear and whatever it was that Tooth was, was immense, slamming each other against the rock face. The bear's claws swiped away at Tooth's flannel and then the flesh he wore beneath and he grabbed at the creature's eyes trying to blind it. Rubble fell around the monsters as they continued to collide with each other tearing at flesh and fur in a bloodthirsty rage.

As they fell into the cave together it appeared that Tooth was on top and he slipped a hunting knife from the inside of his boot and drove it into the torso of the bear. The bear roared and staggered against the cave wall but Tooth turned to Sheriff Russell and only had eyes for him, he stepped forward as if to leave the bear wounded and go back for the man, but there was a huge ear splitting sound that caused the Sheriff to fall on his backside. He gazed up not knowing what the sound was and the sky was filled with a thick red mist as a flaming flare lodged itself into the rock face above the cave and a heavy avalanche of snow and rubble fell down around the entrance to the cave.

Agnes stood holding the flare gun and Sheriff Russell smiled at her as they both sighed with relief as snow and rock fell down and covered up the cave, the last thing they witnessed was the bear rising up and wrapping his clawed arms around Beau Tooth.

"Agnes!" Sheriff Russell said as he began to weep and laugh at the same time.

"I was aiming for his head." She scoffed and threw away the flare gun and met the Sheriff in the snow as they knelt together and held each other crying and laughing together as the last rock fell in front of the cave, trapping the evil inside.

"Thank you." Agnes said.

"For what? You saved the day."

"But you came for me. You made it right. In my eyes you have back your honour and your identity."

They held each other tightly and weeped loudly, Agnes felt his strong arms and the ripe smell of his manly sweat and thought of her brother. Patrick felt her hair against his face and thought about his wife it was a perfect moment for closure and as the two parted and wiped tears away from their eyes they smiled at each other.

"I have my honour and identity back." He grinned proudly.

"I can't give you love." Agnes said.

"Nor would I ask that of you."

"But you do have my respect."

The pair hugged again and there was a howling sound and a bark that for a second sent a chill down both of their spines as Nora bounded towards the pair and jumped up at Patrick licking at his face lovingly.

"I think you have found someone who can fill that void for you, Sheriff." She laughed and Nora leapt at her too and lathered her in damp kisses.

CHAPTER 33

Mack had neglected his snow ploughing duties and as soon as he had seen Lieutenant Adams back to the Sheriff's Office safe he had returned to Maple Cross. He found the exasperated pair of Sheriff Russell and Agnes Duckworth shuffling along the side of the road, with Nora hot on their heels.

When they arrived back in town the office had things under control with areas that had been affected by the carnage cordoned off, locals being spoken to by Sergeant Church while Officer Smith was busy ushering ambulances and fire crews that had been sent urgently from the nearby towns of Crimson and Haast. The local fire crew had dealt with the fires and Sheriff Russell watched on as black plumes of smoke bellowed out from buildings and vehicles.

Nora ran away down a nearby alleyway to lap water out of an upturned garbage can lid, she drank feverishly, as if suffering from a raging thirst.

Lieutenant Adams was in the middle of the town taking command, she had finished taking notes from Drunken

Donald and patted him on the back and sent him on his way, apparently his statement had said that he was never going to drink again. Her eyes met Sheriff Russell's and they shimmered with moisture but her face blushed with relief and she smiled. Agnes found some energy from somewhere and ran to embrace the Lieutenant and the pair hugged tightly and shared tears of joy and relief.

Sheriff Russell smiled and watched the moment play out as Adams led her to the back of a nearby ambulance where she was checked over by a paramedic.

Other scenes were not as pleasant as a black body bag was wheeled out of *Chopper's Bar* on a trolley through the uneven terrain of snow and placed in the rear of an ambulance.

The Sheriff sighed and dropped his head.

"Goodbye my old friend." He whispered into the night, hoping the words caught the wind and took them to wherever the old man was, "I did what I said. I got him."

An officer walked past with the head of Wendy Hardwood in a thick plastic bag, Sheriff Russell was thankful for the bag's thickness for it obscured the view of what horror was concealed within.

He drew his eyes away and jumped out his skin as a paramedic touched his arm and asked him if he needed any medical attention, but he waved her away believing there were others who needed help more than him.

The charred body of Officer Scott Ouellet was dragged out of the burnt out wreckage of the Volkswagen Beetle and twisted steel of what was once a Bobcat snowmobile. His heart broke into pieces of shrapnel and pierced his vital organs within when he saw them slide the blackened burnt flesh of his body into a black bag.

He closed his eyes and it was as if it was the worst thing he could have done, because he saw the faces of the dead as clear as day. He had tried not to take in those lying dead and frozen on Tooth's sledge back at The Cross, but they had left their haunting mark on his mind's eye with just one glance and would no doubt torment his dreams for the rest of his days. The thought of poor Raymond Clegg's glazed eyes staring at him as if they were about to leak tears churned his stomach and he thought to himself that Raymond wouldn't like the dark.

Sheriff Russell opened his eyes, he had to, releasing a huge sigh, his chest felt as though it had caved in under the pressure of such loss.

"You're alive." Adams said, approaching him with a smile.

"So are you."

"Mack, tells me I have you to thank for that."

309

"Just doing my job." He shrugged, but looked away shyly.

"Well, thank you all the same." She said with a roll of her eyes and kissed him on his cheek.

He was taken aback by it and although the sensation was a warming one against his cold cheek he couldn't help but feel embarrassed and uncomfortable and he stepped away from her with a shy smile.

"Ask them if they have some more bags because there's a sledge full of bodies out there on The Cross."

Tammy watched him walk away, an uncomfortable yearning gripped her heart and squeezed it, but she was ever the professional.

"I'll get onto it right away." She said as she watched him walk away from her.

"We got a live one here!" Shouted a paramedic and Sheriff Russell was pleased to see Dawn Rougeau being wheeled out on a gurney and oxygen mask strapped to her face.

"Dawn! You're okay!" he said, meeting her as they wheeled through the snow, she sat up and grabbed the mask, pulling it away from her mouth and smiled a crooked smile, breaths spluttered from her maw in staggered bursts.

"Tell me you got the son of a bitch. Tell me you did..."

He nodded and smiled.

"We got him, Dawn."

He held her hand and gave it a squeeze.

"Thank God!" She said, collapsing back into the gurney and sliding the mask back on as tears rolled down her cheeks. He watched as they wheeled her away and gazed around at his broken community, questions would be asked by those that dwell there about its safety and he would have to answer those questions and reassure those worries.

That was his job.

His crew looked tired and distraught, but did their jobs to the best of their abilities. He had lost good people and good friends and again it would be left to him to regroup and recruit a new generation of officers to help keep the town safe. A task that many would now no doubt find an undesirable assignment.

"Regroup, rebuild and start over." He said to himself. They were wise words he knew, because they weren't his. His predecessor Sheriff Windwood had once said something similar to him when he first arrived. It had been his job to recruit the last time but now he knew the truth as to why they were low on officers. Tooth had taken them and to not scare the town Windwood had covered it up.

Sheriff Russell knew there was much to do and it wasn't over yet, there was still a long way to go to rebuild what had been destroyed by that monster, the lives he had taken would leave deep wounds on the town for years to come but together he knew they could overcome it.

He gave Lieutenant Adams a nod as he limped up the high street, she had it under control he knew and his pillow was calling. He gave a quick whistle and Nora joined him at his side and unbeknownst to him Tammy Adams watched him leave with the new lady in his life and cursed herself for being jealous of a dog.

"You coming home with me Nora?" Russell asked and she replied with a bark.

"I hope you don't snore." He said with a chuckle and she made some growling sound and took off at speed running ahead of him excitedly.

He stopped for a moment and turned to gaze up at the mountains in the distance, surrounded by the peaks of trees as the snow fell. He could hear the distant grinding of the snowplough as it drove along Maple Cross sifting snow out of its way, it was a distant sound, an unusual sound, like the sound of growling. For a moment it sounded as though it could have been the sound of a bear locked in a desperate clinch with a monster.

THE END

THE WORKS OF DANIEL J. BARNES

Secret Hunters Horde: Cursed Convent
Secret Hunters Horde: Monster Home
Secret Hunters Horde: Finding Condor
Vatican: Angel of Justice
Vatican: Retribution
Vatican: Unholy Alliance
Hartwaker: The End of Kings
Hartwaker: A Slayer's Quest
Blood Stained Canvas
Maple Falls Massacre
Maple Falls Massacre 2: Sacrificial Lambs
Fear Trigger
Welcome to Crimson
Dinner Party
Dupliicate
Magpa: Sorrow

CHILDREN'S BOOKS

Monster Meals
Eatington: Brave Banana
Eatington: Creative Carrot
Eatington: Learn the Alphabet

Follow author Daniel J.Barnes on social media
@DJBWriter on Facebook, Instagram & Twitter.

Printed in Great Britain
by Amazon